Uncle Robert's Secret

Illustrated by Frank Aloise

Uncle Robert's Secret

Wylly Folk St. John

A CAMELOT BOOK / PUBLISHED BY AVON BOOKS

AVON BOOKS
A division of
The Hearst Corporation
959 Eighth Avenue
New York, New York 10019

ISBN: 0-380-00909-9

First Camelot Printing, February, 1977

Printed in the U.S.A.

*This book, with love,
is for the real Bob and Debbi and Sonny*

WYLLY FOLK ST. JOHN is a true Southerner. She was born in South Carolina, spent her childhood in Savannah, graduated from the University of Georgia in Athens, and is now living in Social Circle, not far from Atlanta. She was employed as a staff writer for the Magazine Section of the *Atlanta Journal and Constitution* for many years.

CONTENTS

THE RESCUE

My brother Bob had a secret. The kind of secret that would get him in trouble for sure.

But he couldn't keep it a secret from us. He had to let Sonny and me in on it because we had already discovered what it was the day after Mama and Dad left for Oklahoma—at least we knew part of it, the part he thought he was keeping hidden from everybody, down in the basement playroom. What we didn't know was *why*. And where the secret came from. And how in the world he was going to keep it hidden. That could have been his real problem, even with Sonny and me helping him—which he knew we'd do if only he let us in on it. Later he said he had meant to tell us all the time, even if we hadn't found out.

I'm eleven and a half and Sonny's nine. That makes me and Sonny together nearly twice as smart as Bob by himself, because he's only thirteen. And besides, girls mature earlier, as Mama says when she wants me to do something Bob is supposed to do. So he really did the best thing, getting us to help him keep anybody else from finding out.

I had made a guess at why Bob had the secret, but it didn't really make sense that he'd go that far. You see, I thought—though I was only partly right—I thought it was because he wanted so bad to be Uncle Robert.

I myself wasn't so crazy about the idea that I was going to be Aunt Debbi—I'm too young to be an aunt, really. And Sonny couldn't have cared less about the fact that our older sister Betsy was going to have a baby. But when Betsy started going to the Red Cross classes—way back when she thought being pregnant was so great and exciting—to learn about taking care of a baby, she asked Bob if he didn't want to go too so he could learn to baby-sit for her. She was kidding, but Bob did it. The Red Cross actually let him. He took it all so seriously that we had to laugh. It was all very well for Betsy's husband Joe to go; he was involved in the baby, being its father. But we couldn't imagine old Bob putting a diaper on a doll. (He didn't tell us that part; Joe did.) Of course they don't let them practice on a real baby. But I even pitied the doll.

When the Red Cross wouldn't give Bob a certificate for knowing how to take care of babies, Betsy fixed him one herself. She typed it and put a seal on it with her sealing wax. And when we all laughed (Mama too), Betsy hugged him and said, "Uncle Bob's going to be a great baby sitter."

Bob got all solemn and puffed up, feeling important.

He said, "I don't intend for him to call me Uncle Bob. He's going to call me Uncle Robert." So Betsy said O.K. and hugged him again. She didn't hug me and Sonny, but we didn't promise to baby-sit for her either.

Then before the baby was due, Joe got transferred, and he and Betsy moved out to Oklahoma. And that did Uncle Robert out of anybody to call him Uncle.

In July, a month before the baby was supposed to be born, Joe got hurt in a car smashup. That was the reason Mama and Dad had to go out there. Betsy phoned from the hospital and scared Mama to death, being hysterical, but we didn't blame Betsy for being shook up. She was alone, about to have a baby too early in a new place where she didn't know anybody, and her husband was already in the hospital unconscious. Dad was climbing the wall, he was so worried about Betsy, and Mama didn't have the heart to tell him she could handle it by herself. Dad said he'd take a week of his vacation right then and go too.

So they put it up to us: would we let our great-aunts Emma and Cammie come and stay with us while our parents flew out to be with Betsy, and would we be good and not give the old ladies any trouble? The aunts were the only ones they could get to come right then.

Of course we said yes, even though it's the other way around; it's the aunts who always give *us* trouble. They lose their glasses all the time, and they're both practically deaf, so we have to holler and tell Aunt Emma what Aunt Cammie says, and then holler back Aunt Emma's answer. And Aunt Emma has arthritis, which is what old ladies who can't go up and down stairs have—except if it's foot trouble, like hammertoes, which is what Aunt Cammie has. I don't know how they ever manage when they are in their own house on the other side of town and they don't have us to do things for them.

Lucky for Bob they couldn't very well get down to the playroom! Or hear what went on down there either. But of course sitters never could keep up with what we were doing, even sitters lots younger than the aunts.

It was just after Mama and Dad had phoned to tell us that the baby was a girl they had named Michelle and that Betsy and the baby and Joe were all doing O.K. that Bob decided to tell us the secret. At the time I was up in my oak tree, trying to spy on Mr. Peregrine next door.

We live in a small town not far from Atlanta. Nearly all the houses except those right downtown around the courthouse square have an acre or two of back yard. Most of the lots were parts of old family estates that were cut up and sold for houses a long time ago, Mama says. The lots are all great big ones, so you can even keep a horse in your back yard if you want to. We want to, but so far no luck in getting Mama and Dad to want to.

Our house and Mr. Peregrine's aren't real close together, but luckily my oak tree grows by the stone wall that goes all around his field and yard right up to both sides of his big old house. The wall has only one gate, around on the other side where the alley is and the garbage men come. The gate's kept locked, but I guess he unlocks it when he puts out his garbage. We don't even have a fence around our place.

The great thing about Mr. Peregrine's property is the spooky old family cemetery in his field. There's a little iron fence around it. It's right under some of the limbs of my oak tree that hang over the wall. In the old days there was a lot of dying, and some people had their own graveyards, Mama says, because there weren't too many churches, and preachers only came around once in a while. So they would bury their own dead, and when a preacher came, sometimes a year or two later, he'd read a service over the grave.

From my tree I could read some of the names on the old stones, and none of them was *Peregrine*. Aunt Emma told Mama that Mr. Peregrine's house had been the old Stanford place (Mr. Peregrine's grandmother was a Stanford) since before the Civil War, and sure enough some of the gravestones had *Stanford* on them, and the dates were back in the 1800s. Some of the stones were so old, and gray and green with moss, that you couldn't read the names at all, and only parts of the verses on them. But there was one grave I had always been curious about. It looked a little bit newer than the others, and I could read everything on the marker, even though I'd never had the nerve actually to climb over into Mr. Peregrine's yard.

The marker was pretty old, too, of course, though not as old looking as the Stanford tombstones. There was no name on it—only the initials *M.C.* and no *S* for Stanford. The date was no more than a year, 1932.

Then there was lettering, and as near as I could make it out, all it said was *God Will Judge. Heb. 13:4.*

So of course we wondered all the time about M.C. and why God will judge. Well, maybe not all the time, but every now and then when the subject came up.

Mr. Peregrine had bought the house about sixty or so years ago, Aunt Cammie told Mama, so he'd lived there long enough for it to be called the Peregrine place instead of the Stanford place, I'd have thought. But that's the way it is around here—the houses are all called by somebody else's name. We Howards, for instance, live at the old Malcom place. Dad had had the house completely remodeled when he bought it, so it didn't look old and crummy like Mr. Peregrine's did, with its funny gables and balconies and no paint left and trees that never got trimmed.

We've only lived here about three years; we had lived for a couple of years before that in the old Howard place with Dad's Aunt Emma and Aunt Cammie. It was awful old, too, but it didn't have a family graveyard, I'm sorry to say. And it wasn't as spooky looking as Mr. Peregrine's.

I had asked Mama why Mr. Peregrine had the wall all around his yard—was he maybe trying to hide something? She'd said she suspected it was something he was trying to hide *from* that made him put up a wall between himself and the rest of the world. But she wouldn't tell me what she meant by that. Mama heard more gossip than we did, and a lot more than she told us.

Mr. Peregrine was an interesting-looking old man, at

least as old as the aunts. Whenever we saw him come out of his front door—only a couple of times a week—we always followed him, making sure he couldn't see us, thinking he might lead us to his den of thieves or whatever he had that was so mysterious. But so far he hadn't gone anywhere but to the grocery store and once to the doctor's office.

He was tall and skinny with thin white hair and lots of wrinkles in his face. He always wore a black suit and a white shirt with a little black necktie that he tied in a bow. Mama called it a string tie. The aunts had told her he used to be a minister but something happened to him and he quit preaching. He had a gold watch chain across his vest, and he carried a walking stick. We thought he probably had plenty of money—he didn't look poor or anything, and he sent his laundry out. The kids at school said he kept all his money—a whole bunch of money—hidden somewhere in his house because he didn't believe in banks.

Whenever Mama said, "Good morning, Mr. Peregrine," he always took off that broad-brimmed black hat of his and said, "Good morning, Mrs. Howard." But he never said it's a nice day or anything. He just went on down the street or back inside his house. We somehow got the idea that he didn't like children. Mama told us not to bother him, and we didn't.

But my oak tree was a lot higher than his old stone wall; so we could keep an eye on what went on in his back yard and in the field behind it, too. Not that anything much did, at least before this time that Mama and Dad were away. Things began to happen then.

I was up in my tree and our cat Gibson was over in Mr. Peregrine's yard, stalking a field mouse or something in all those weeds in his flower bed. Sonny was climbing a few branches below me. I was watching Gibson and just getting ready to call him when Bob came out of the basement door and wandered over to the tree and said, "Debbi, you want to know a secret?"

"Well, sure," I said, "but I better get Gibson back over here first. I don't think Mr. Peregrine likes cats any better than he likes children. Here, Gibson, here, kitty kitty kitty—" Gibson is a big black he-man tomcat, but he comes when I call him. I'm the one who usually feeds him.

Sonny said, "I do! I want to know the secret, Bob!"

Bob said, "Yes, you too, Sonny," but he didn't say any more till we were both down from the tree and I had Gibson in my arms.

I said, "What's up?"

"Come with me," Bob said mysteriously. I knew he was going to take us to the playroom, but I waited to see how he was going to explain about what he had there.

Sonny said, "We saw—" but I gave him The Look and he shut up. Gibson didn't want to stay with us, so I let him go.

As he took us in Bob said, "Don't make any extra noise down here, because I don't want the aunts wondering."

"Aw, they couldn't even hear it if we set off my dynamite," Sonny said. He had found something he thought was dynamite. We didn't exactly know what dynamite looked like, but Bob and I didn't think that was it or we wouldn't have let him keep it.

The playroom is almost the whole basement, but only one side of it is finished. Dad plans to work on it some more when he has time. Now it just has our old TV set, a rug and sofa Mama wanted to get rid of, Sonny's tropical fish tank, and of course the maid's room and bathroom, in case we had a maid, which we don't. There are lots of our toys and things down there because Mama likes to keep them out of the way. It's a great place to play on a rainy day, and we build things and keep our collections and stuff down there. Bob even keeps his animal bones and his grandfather turtle shell in one corner, and the smell doesn't bother Mama except when she comes down to do the laundry. In fact we can do just about anything we please in the playroom—it's sort of our territory. There are steps coming down from the back hall, and another door to the back yard.

It didn't look any different from usual when Bob opened the door, but he shut it behind us and then said, "O.K., Tim, you can come out now."

Nothing happened.

Bob said, "He was right here—" He ran over to the maid's room, and we followed. Mama had put a bed in there once when she thought she might get a maid. Bob's secret was lying on it, asleep.

He was a little kid. I mean little. Not much bigger than a baby. About three years old maybe, but so skinny and hunched up you couldn't really tell. He looked kind of pathetic, and for a minute I didn't get

why that was. Then I realized he looked like that starved alley cat we fed one time before we got Gibson. He looked all skin and bones. He had reddish hair, and his pants and shirt were awfully dirty. One side of his face had a great big blue bruise on it. So did his arm and one leg. And there was blood on his shirt. One arm was around the dirtiest little old stuffed rabbit I ever saw.

That morning Sonny and I hadn't had time to see much about how he looked, because Bob had shut the door so fast. Then the aunts had made us come to lunch. Of course we couldn't talk to Bob about it in front of them, and after lunch he had checked out before we could ask him anything. When we tried the basement door it was locked. From the inside. And he wouldn't answer when we called him.

But now he had realized he needed us. Three are lots better than one.

Sonny said, "Where'd he come from?"

"Did you kidnap him, Bob?" I asked. "What for?" The kid didn't look like much of a prize, and it's against the law to hold anybody for ransom anyway.

"Well, kind of," Bob answered. "Not really."

"Level with us," I said.

"Come on out here where we won't wake him up." Sonny and I took the sofa and Bob sat on the hassock in front of us.

"Does he call you Uncle Robert?" Sonny said in his sweet-sarcastic voice. Bob didn't answer that one.

"Here's the whole thing," Bob said seriously. "This kid has a mother and father you wouldn't believe. I was down at the edge of the woods early this morning —you know, over there where I found the cow skull and those great old rib bones—and I heard some yelling and screaming going on in that shack we wondered who lived in. I sneaked up close and looked through a big knothole. There was a man, hitting this kid with a belt—with the buckle end of it—and a woman, who wasn't doing a thing to stop him. The kid was crying, of course, and I was just about to run and get the police when they decided to go off somewhere in an old car they had. They tied this kid to the bed with some rope and went off and left him. As soon as I could I untied him. He was crying like he'd never stop and hanging onto me. And he followed me when I started to leave, just like that poor old cat did that time. So I brought him home on my bike. Lucky nobody was looking when we got here. He says his name is Tim, but he can't talk very well. I asked him the names of the mean man and woman, and he said their names are Daddy and Mama."

"That's awful," I said. "I never would have thought a mother and father could hurt their kid like that. Are we going to call the police, Bob?"

"I don't know. I guess we ought to. But I'd kind of like to keep him for a day or two and—"

"And let him call you Uncle Robert?" Sonny said innocently.

Bob ignored him. "Naturally I mean to tell the police sometime," he said, "because those two ought to be put in jail. But then what would happen to Tim? An orphans' home, that's what. I wish we could wait till Dad and Mama get back, at least. I sneaked some milk and crackers and stuff down here after lunch, and you ought to have seen him eat! He could stay right here and nobody would know."

"He sure needs taking care of," I said. "As soon as he wakes up let's give him a bath. I'll see if I can find something he can wear. I wonder if any of Sonny's old clothes are small enough. Maybe I could take them up some and they'd do."

"You're real good at sewing, Debbi," Bob said. "See what you can fix for him, will you?"

"Sure," I said, though I knew he was just saying that to get me to do it. He doesn't really think my sewing is all that good. "And of course we can wash the clothes he has on."

"But won't those people be looking for him?" Sonny said.

"I don't think they really want him," Bob said. "They'd probably be glad to get rid of him."

He was wrong; it turned out they did want him pretty bad. But we didn't find out why they needed him until later.

We heard the kid waking up then, sort of crying. Sure enough, when Bob went in there we heard something that sounded like "Uncle Wobert." Sonny looked like he was about to make another crack about it, but I told him to lay off. I could understand kind of how Bob felt about that. When you are so awfully disappointed like he was about Betsy's baby, you don't need anybody to tease you about it.

Bob came out leading the kid by the hand. "Tim,"

he said, "this is Debbi and this is Sonny. When I'm not here, you do what they tell you, O.K.?"

"O.K.," Tim said. His eyes were blue and round.

Sonny and I said, "Hello, Tim," and I went and started a bath in the maid's tub, because you can't hug a kid with any enthusiasm till he is cleaner than that one was. "Take off his clothes, Bob," I said.

Bob did, and Sonny said, "Doesn't he know how to go to the bathroom?"

"Of course he does," Bob said, "but you'd wet your

pants too if anybody had hit you with a belt like that. Just look at these cuts on his back!" He turned Tim around, and his back was all red and kind of cut up.

"I'll be careful not to hurt you, Tim," I promised, holding out my hands to him. "Come on and get in the tub. The warm water'll feel good, and then we'll get some medicine to put on the bad places, and some clean clothes." He hung onto Bob, so I said, "Well, Bob, you bathe him while I go look for clothes, and Sonny, you get some Mercurochrome and that tube of first-aid ointment out of the upstairs bathroom."

"What do I say if the aunts ask me what I want with it?"

"Tell them you need it for me. If they keep on about it, just pretend you're answering—you know, move your mouth—and they'll think they just can't hear you." I do that lots of times, and it works. The aunts don't like to admit how hard of hearing they are.

I went to the utility room and found some old clothes of Sonny's that Mama had put in the rag bag. She gives the good ones to the welfare people, but these were too far gone to give away. They'd do for Tim till we could wash what he had on. His own clothes weren't much better than Sonny's old ones, though, I found out when we went to wash them. He looked right funny in Sonny's pants and shirt, which were too big, but we pinned up the pants with safety pins, and at least he looked clean. Bob said Tim didn't even cry when he put the medicine on the sore places. "Just think how we'd feel if our Dad ever hurt us like that," he said.

I couldn't imagine it. Dad never even spanked us, not even when we did something awful. But I think I'd rather be spanked than have him look disappointed in me or give me The Lecture.

Mama and Dad are pretty reasonable though and usually see our side of whatever happens. Also, they think things are funny. If we can make them laugh, we know it's O.K.

"I think I've made Tim understand that he's supposed to stay down here and not make any noise, and we'll come as often as we can and bring him things to eat," Bob said. "He's scared his father will find him, so I guess he'll keep quiet. But it'll be safer if we lock the outside door and the one at the foot of the inside steps, too."

"He'll be pretty lonesome," I said. "One of us ought to stay with him as much as we can."

"I'll leave the TV on," Bob said. "Tim, you like to watch the cartoons?"

I guess he never had been able to watch the cartoons before. He sat there in front of the set like he was glued down, and he never took his eyes off that junk. They do old cartoons over and over, and we had quit watching them a long time ago.

"I hope that stupid cat won't make him scared of Gibson," Sonny said when Sylvester came on the screen trying to gobble up Tweetie.

I put the clothes in the dryer and we left Tim with the cartoons while we went to supper. The aunts couldn't hear the TV going in the basement.

I thought about taking a blanket down there after

supper, but it was so warm I decided Tim wouldn't need it. I just took clean sheets and a pillow. Good thing it was summer. It's lots easier to dress a kid for warm weather.

After supper Bob got caught fixing up a plate of pot roast and creamed potatoes and gravy and had to tell Aunt Emma it was for Gibson. "You mean that cat eats potatoes?" she said. "Well, now, I want to see that! I never in my life saw a cat that would eat potatoes. Did you, Cammie?"

Of course Aunt Cammie had to have it all shouted to her, and then she wanted to see Gibson eat potatoes too. Naturally Gibson turned up his nose at the potatoes after he had eaten all the meat and gravy. "I knew it," Aunt Emma said triumphantly. "I knew cats don't eat potatoes!"

But while they were watching Gibson, Bob had fixed up another plate behind their backs, and Sonny and I were trying to keep from laughing because he was mocking the way Aunt Emma bent over to see Gibson and the way Aunt Cammie poked the potatoes at him. Bob waved a fork at us and left just before Gibson sat down to lick his paws and wash his face.

"I think I'll have another glass of milk," I said, "to take outside to drink while I watch the lightning bugs."

"What did you say, dear?" Aunt Emma asked.

"She said she was going to catch lightning bugs, sister," Aunt Cammie said. "But I didn't know you could catch them with milk, Debbi."

"Not catch them, watch them!" I hollered, but it

was no use. "Never mind, Aunt Cammie," I said. "Sonny"—I spoke very low so they couldn't hear me—"when they get out of the kitchen, you bring some ice cream on down." And what do you know? They heard what I said! That's the trouble with deaf aunts. You can't ever be quite sure what they'll hear and what they won't. Dad says they're only deaf north-north-west.

"If you children want ice cream," Aunt Emma said primly, "eat it at the table. Dessert after the table's cleared, please, Debbi." So I had to clear the table before I could get away with the milk for Tim.

"No, ma'am, we don't want any ice cream," I said. "May we be excused?"

"But you said you wanted ice cream," Aunt Cammie said.

"Never mind. Please excuse us, Aunt Cammie? Aunt Emma?"

"Very well. Go catch your lightning bugs with your milk, then. But I'm certain you'll find it's just like the cat and the potatoes. Lightning bugs won't drink milk, Debbi."

"Boy, is she confused!" Sonny said when we escaped, carrying the milk. But Tim would have to wait for his ice cream till the aunts got settled on the front porch.

It still wasn't quite dark—you know that pretty time when the sun's just down and the sky is kind of on fire behind the trees, and even the air is pink. I sat on the front steps to fool the aunts until it was safe to go through the front yard and around to the back where the basement door is. Sonny was with me, and pretty soon Bob came and sat on the bottom step, too.

"He's eating," Bob said, low enough so the aunts couldn't hear. "Poor little guy. I'm not going to turn him over to the police right now, Debbi. I've made up my mind. They'd put him in some old home or something till they could decide what to do about his father's beating him up. I'm going to keep him right here till Dad and Mama come home. I bet they won't blame me. Maybe they'll let us keep him when those no-good child-beaters go to jail."

"O.K.," I said, and Sonny nodded. "But won't he be scared to sleep down there by himself? He's pretty little."

"I'll sneak down and sleep with him after the aunts go to bed," Bob said. "He won't be afraid if I'm there. He thinks I'm grown up."

"That kid has a lot to learn," Sonny said.

"You shut up," I told Sonny. "Bob's right. You just think how you'd feel if you were in Tim's place."

"Aw, I didn't mean anything," Sonny said. "I'm sorry for him, too. But I don't think I need another brother."

"I guess I'd better catch a lightning bug with this milk," I said. "Aunt Cammie's watching." And we all giggled. The aunts like to sit on the porch after supper, either at their own house or when they're at ours.

Sonny said, "I'll catch some," and he ran out on the front lawn.

I started to get up with the glass of milk, but Bob said suddenly, intensely, "There he is!"

"Who?"

He crooked his arm over his face. "Debbi—he must have found out! He's after the poor little guy—or me! But I was sure they didn't see me . . ."

There was a man walking along in front of our house, but of course there's a wide lawn between the road and the steps where we were.

"Who? Him?" I sat down again. It was just an ordinary guy walking past, dressed in blue slacks and a plaid sport shirt. "Him?"

Bob said, low but kind of excited and still hiding his face, "That's the one. I'm sure of it. He's got a mean look I couldn't possibly forget. Debbi, that's the man who was beating Tim this morning!"

THE CHASE

"You're putting me on," I said. "He couldn't have found out if he didn't even see you. And besides—you can look now, Bob—he's already gone past our house."

Bob cautiously uncovered his face. The man hadn't even glanced at us. We watched while he walked past our hedge and started along beside Mr. Peregrine's wall. Once he touched it with his hand, and once he looked up as if he were measuring with his eyes how high it was.

Then we saw something really unbelievable. He was turning in at Mr. Peregrine's.

"He's got the wrong house, that's all," said Bob.

"No. He doesn't know anything about you. He's just going to see Mr. Peregrine."

"What could he be doing that for? Nobody ever goes to see Mr. Peregrine. And anyway, Mr. Peregrine wouldn't let him in," Bob said.

"He probably wouldn't even hear the doorbell. He usually sits out by his back door for a while after supper." I knew he didn't do anything but sit in one of his old canvas chairs and smoke his pipe. He didn't even read the paper. I'd watched him lots of times. He looked awfully lonesome.

One of us was right—either he didn't want to answer the doorbell or he didn't hear it. After a few minutes the man came down Mr. Peregrine's steps and walked on, heading the other way.

"Let's follow him!" I said. We were allowed to play outside till nine in the summer; the aunts wouldn't miss us.

"We'll have to tell Sonny to stay with Tim and give him his milk and ice cream. I tell you what, Debbi—you start after that guy and just barely keep him in sight till I can brief Sonny and then catch up with you." We had agreed that all of us shouldn't ever be away from the house at the same time as long as Tim was locked in the playroom; in case of a fire nobody would know to rescue him.

"Right." We got up casually and strolled out into the yard. I handed Bob the glass of milk behind the cape jasmine bush so the aunts wouldn't see, and then I slipped along out of sight beside the high hedge until I figured I was far enough from the porch to walk as usual on the side of the road. I lingered way back from the man, just barely keeping him in sight, and of course he had no idea he was being followed. Bob caught up with me pretty soon.

"No trouble with Sonny?"

"I didn't give him time to object. He was kind of interested in the western on TV anyhow. He and Tim

will probably still be watching it when we get back. I told Sonny to go up the back way and get them both some ice cream at the next commercial and to keep the door locked and not pay any attention to the aunts."

"I wonder what in the world Tim's dad went to Mr. Peregrine's for," I said as we kept on following him.

"Me too."

He didn't do anything very suspicious, it was a very dull bit of following. He walked on past Stephen Lee's and some more of our friends' houses and then went by the Institute for the Deaf. It's a school where they keep the deaf-and-dumb kids and try to teach them to talk. None of the kids was on the playground, though.

We kind of pretended the suspect was about to notice us, and we dodged behind trees along the side of the road and sometimes took to the shrubbery for a few minutes; but he really didn't have any idea we were interested in him. In a little while Bob said, "He's just going to his shack, that's all. I guess his car must be out of gas or something."

"Well, it's not very far. Just a nice little walk, on the edge of the woods part of the way. Maybe he's a bird watcher."

"No, bird watchers are nice people. He's definitely not a nice person."

It was the same walk we always took when we were going to see Mrs. McHenny. She lived in another little tumble-down house not too far from where Bob had found the cow bones. People who don't have proper houses like ours seem to get along almost as well as the ones who do. And they have a lot more free time. They don't always have to be cleaning up the way Mama does in case somebody should drop in, or fixing flower arrangements because the bridge club's coming, or things like that. They don't have any rugs to shampoo. When Dad's off from the TV station in Atlanta, where he's a news broadcaster, he has to mow the lawn and trim the hedge and all. Mrs. McHenny doesn't have any husband now, but she doesn't need one—she doesn't have any lawn or hedge either.

She used to have three husbands—one at a time, of course. When I asked her what they were like, she said, "Various." One turned out to have had another wife someplace. He was a shade-tree mechanic. That's somebody, she told us, who doesn't have a mechanic's shop but fixes things under a tree in his back yard. The second went off and left her, and she had him declared. That means after seven years she got a judge to say he was officially and legally dead whether he was or not, so she'd be free to remarry. But her third, Mr. McHenny—she calls him Mr. Mac—was an angel to her for the six years he survived after they got married. Then he went to his reward. He used to bring her breakfast in bed. Two glasses of it, she says, "a second helping of hair of the dog." I guess that means beer, in her case. Her husbands were pretty various, all right.

But she's a very jolly lady, and we like her. Maybe that's because she likes us. She used to baby-sit for us sometimes, before Mama found out that she drank. We usually go by to see her when we're out that way.

"Let's say hello to Mrs. McHenny on the way back," Bob said.

"Right. Bob, should we tell her about Tim?"

Bob considered. "I don't know," he said doubtfully. "I kind of think the fewer people who know a secret, the better it is. Of course Mrs. McHenny wouldn't tell if we asked her not to, but—well, she talks a lot, especially when she's just got her government check and has a lot of beer on hand. Maybe we won't tell her yet. Of course if we should need some advice or something, she'd be a good one to ask. But let's wait till we need her."

"She must be home—there's a light in her kitchen."

"Well, it's nowhere near really dark yet. We'll have time to stop in for a minute on the way back."

Tim's father's shack was farther off the main drag than Mrs. McHenny's, down a dirt road that led into the woods. It was darker under the trees, but we had seen him turn in and we went in behind him. We knew he'd be inside the house before we reached it, so he probably wouldn't see us. But we were cautious anyhow. We really didn't have any excuse for being there if he should catch us, and there wasn't any place else we could be going.

Bob said, as if he had guessed what I was thinking, "Well, I did find the cow bones near here. We could be looking for some more bones."

"Hardly anybody would believe that."

"Well, if I'm going to be an archaeologist or a paleontologist I have to do research, don't I? Real paleontologists and archaeologists work all night sometimes, if they're hot on a project. I bet Schliemann didn't stop for supper or anything when he was looking for Helen of Troy's bones."

"Well, you tell it if we get caught. I might laugh."

"Don't knock it for an excuse. It's all we've got."

"He probably won't catch us, if we're careful."

"The windows are open," Bob pointed out. "If we can get close enough to see and hear . . ."

"Good thing there are a lot of bushes. He doesn't bother to trim them even next to the house."

We slipped in close, and there was a lighted window that we could almost see into, but not quite. We

looked around among all the junk scattered about for
something to stand on, but nothing looked useful except maybe an old washtub that was leaning against
the shed. Bob motioned to it, and we each took a
handle and brought it under the window, turning it
over and trying not to make a sound. It wasn't easy—
metal stuff makes more noise than anything else, I've
noticed.

He whispered, "We'll need to get on it at the same
time, or it might tilt."

We each put a foot on it and then, carefully, holding
the side of the house, hoisted ourselves close together
on the tub's upturned bottom. Now we could see into
the window.

The woman was saying, "You didn't see him anywhere? I've been looking ever since I got home, and
he's not around here."

The man told her, "He couldn't have gone far. Don't
worry about him. Worry about why I couldn't get the
old man to answer the door."

She said, "Well, I guess you can't make him see
you." She had long muddy blond hair. She wasn't very
pretty. All of a sudden I was glad Mama made me
brush my own hair a hundred strokes every night.
Probably Tim's mother didn't know about doing that.
And I was glad mine was pale blond instead of ugly
like hers.

When I took a good look at Tim's father I saw what
Bob meant about his face being mean. It was narrow
and his eyes were set close together, and he hadn't
shaved very well. After about a minute I realized

what he reminded me of. He looked sort of like a possum we saw one time in the zoo—if it had had dark hair. A sneaky-looking possum.

"I'm going to get in that house somehow," the man was telling the woman. He had opened a beer and was drinking it in gulps. "Maybe I can sweet-talk him into doing what we planned. That would make it easy, Adele. But if he won't even answer the doorbell and I have to get in some other way, he'll be suspicious."

"He has to come out sometime," Adele said. "We'll have to keep watching, I guess, and catch him when he leaves the house."

"If he'd leave the house I might even get in while he's gone.

"You wouldn't have time to find anything. You'll need a long time to search all over that big old place. You've got to get him to let us stay a while. You can sweet-talk him, Clay."

Now we knew both their names. At least their first names.

"But Clay," Adele went on, "we've got to find Tim." He ignored that, and I was glad he didn't much want to find Tim.

He said, "I guess you're right; we have to get in with the old man. The money ought to be mine, any way you look at it. Maybe if I broke in and then just leveled with him—told him that I couldn't get him to answer the door and that I had to talk to him— Do you figure that would work? Or would he be so mad he wouldn't listen?"

"He might be scared into having a stroke or something," Adele said. "He's pretty old. You don't want anything to happen to him before he can make that will."

"Or change it—if he's made one that's not what we want." Clay opened another beer. Adele held out her hand, and he gave the can to her and got himself another. They didn't use glasses, just drank it out of the cans. Mrs. McHenny always poured hers into a big glass mug that she said Mr. Mac got at a pub in Ireland a long time ago.

"What about Tim?" Adele said again. "How are we going to find him? He's our kid, and we can't just forget about him. You didn't have to beat him like that— maybe we needed to take him to a doctor. I feel terrible when I think about Tim. Besides, we need him for—" She began to cry. Then she took another long drink of beer.

"He'll show up," Clay told her. "He's just hiding somewhere around here. He'll come back when he gets hungry enough."

"Clay, he's just a baby. He'd get lost if he went far from the house. We ought to get the police to look for him. They always hunt for kids that get lost in the woods. They don't charge anything."

"I don't want the police to see—"

I knew what he didn't want the police to see.

"I warned you, Clay," she said. "I told you there are laws against child abuse. Now we can't get them to find our kid because you'll get arrested for beating him. You should at least go out and look for him yourself, like I did. Maybe you could think of places I didn't look. If he stays out there all night he might die or something, and that would look even worse for us. You know he's not coming back as long as he's afraid of another beating. Even a dog would hide—"

"You talk as if you'd never hit him yourself."

"But I don't beat him a lot, like you do. Just when I lose my temper because he won't eat. They can get you for child neglect if the kid's starved, you know. I do try . . ." She sniffled again, but I didn't feel a bit sorry for her. No matter what she said, she just didn't add up to a good mother.

"If he doesn't show up, I'll look for him. I'll look for him! Shut up about it. Right now I've got to figure out how to get in that house—"

We might have heard more of his plans, except that right then the old tub we were standing on gave way. The bottom was nearly rusted out, and our combined weight finally broke through it. We made considerable noise getting our feet out of the thing. The handles clanked a lot when we thrashed around trying to get loose. The rusty metal scratched my legs, but it didn't really hurt. At last we scraped free of it.

We could hear Clay saying, "What's that?" and Adele saying, "Maybe it's Tim trying to get in."

"Just let me get my hands on him!" Clay said. "I'll teach him to run away—" Then we could hear the door opening around the corner from where we were and the woman calling, "Tim!" Bob pulled me to my feet and we dashed for the dirt road.

"Who's that?" the man shouted. "What are you doing around here? Keep off my place, you little—"

He started running after us, but I don't think he could see our faces. Not well enough to recognize us later, I hoped.

Bob was ahead of me. My heart was pounding like mad, and I had a stitch in my side, but I could almost feel that belt buckle on my back, and I ran faster.

It seemed forever before we got to Mrs. McHenny's and flung ourselves against her back door. "Mrs. McHenny! Mrs. McHenny! Let us in, quick!"

THE LIGHT
IN THE YARD NEXT DOOR

We pushed open her kitchen door, stumbling in. After we slammed it behind us and leaned against it, panting, Bob said, "Actually, I don't think he followed us any farther than the edge of the woods. He didn't see us come in here."

"Why did you run, then?" I said.

"Why did you?"

"Because you did, I guess."

Mrs. McHenny was sitting at her kitchen table with her Irish pub mug of beer in front of her and her whittling knife in her hand. She was working on a little bird. She whittled better than anybody. She could make a bird look so real it would almost fool Gibson.

"What have you two been up to?" she asked. "Somebody following you? Is it a game now you're playing?" Her face crinkled up when she smiled at us; she was always glad to see us. She was fat and looked like somebody in a comic strip, and I guess she'd never

brushed her hair a hundred times every night either, but I never minded if hers looked mussed up. It's funny—when you like a person, it doesn't matter too much how she looks, but you turn up your nose if it's somebody you don't like who looks sloppy.

"No," Bob said quickly. "I guess he wasn't following us after all."

"You ran in here like the devil himself was after you," Mrs. McHenny said. "If your mama knew you were down in the woods when it's nearly dark, she'd—"

"Aw, it's a long time till dark, Mrs. McHenny," I said.

"Who were you running from?" Mrs. McHenny kept on. "Some people are so wicked these days, it's not safe for children to be near them. You're supposed to keep away from strangers; you've been told that often enough, Debbi love. Now who did you think was after you?"

We didn't say anything, because we didn't want to tell her, and yet we didn't want to make up a lie.

"What would you say," Mrs. McHenny asked, "if I told you I know it was that no-good sneaky some-body, Mr. Clay Perry, chasing you?"

"How'd you know?" Bob was so surprised he let out that she was right. I just looked at her with my mouth open. She often surprised us, knowing just what we were thinking or what we'd done. She said she had second sight when it came to kids.

"I know a lot," Mrs. McHenny said, and her red-dened blue eyes looked at us as if she really did. She was plenty sharp for her age, which Mama thought was about sixty-five or more. Mrs. McHenny wasn't saying. "For instance, you two were down there trying to see what those people were doing, weren't you? Meddling in somebody else's business. And poor white trash at that. They have rights, too, you know, even if they are doing suspicious things the law ought to know about. Says he's in construction. Huh. Never works a day, that I can see. But you've no right to be

Peeping Toms—and besides, it's not good manners." She and our parents agree about lots of things that either aren't good for us or aren't good manners.

"What's a Peeping Tom?" I asked, though I guessed it was a man named Tom who was peeping into something that was none of his business.

"We weren't really Peeping Toms," Bob told Mrs. McHenny. He likes to show off that he knows lots of stuff because he's always reading. "These people had on all their clothes. Peeping Tom was a man who peeked at Lady Godiva when she rode down the street naked, and all the other people didn't look, because she was doing it for them."

"You want to tell me," I asked him, "why she was doing such a stupid thing for them?"

"Because her husband was taxing the villagers. This was a long time ago, and as the overlord he could do that. Lady Godiva was demonstrating, see, like people do now who want to protest something. She was protesting those taxes the poor folks had to pay so her husband could buy her lots of fine clothes."

"Well, nowadays anybody who looks in other peoples' windows is called a Peeping Tom," Mrs. McHenny said, trimming the wooden bird's beak down to a fine point. "And that's what you were doing."

"Did you see the tub we were standing on, too, in your mind's eye?" I asked. One time she told me she could see things in her mind's eye. I kind of understood what she meant—sometimes my mind has an eye, too. I began to giggle. "It really was funny, Mrs. McHenny. The tub caught us—the tin was rotten and

44

broke—and we could hardly get our legs out of it in time to run away before he saw who we were."

"I know what you were doing, all right," Mrs. Mc-Henny said, and the way she said it I knew she was on our side. "But what I don't know is why you were doing it."

"Because—" I nearly told her, without thinking. But Bob grabbed my arm and said, "We'd better be going now, Debbi. It really will be dark soon, and the aunts will be wondering where we are."

"Your aunts!" Mrs. McHenny said. "Your mama's gone and left those two poor old ladies at the mercy of you three again?"

"Well, see," Bob began, "Mama and Dad had to go to Oklahoma and look after Betsy and bring her and Mickey home with them if Joe will let them come—"

"Maybe Joe can come too if he can't go back to work right away," I said hopefully. I liked Joe much better than the one Betsy started to marry first.

"Back up now!" Mrs. McHenny said. "Are you telling me Betsy's already had that baby? And what about Joe?"

So we had to tell her all about it, including that we had decided we were going to call Michelle "Mickey" for short. Bob was shoving me out the door while we talked. And we left with Mrs. McHenny still exclaiming about it all and making plans to whittle a Noah's ark and a lot of animals for Mickey to play with when she got a little bigger.

I looked around when we left Mrs. McHenny's; I was sort of afraid Clay was waiting out there to jump us as soon as we were in the open again. But nobody seemed to be watching for us. We started running, though. Just because it was getting late.

We hadn't been away longer than two TV programs, though it did seem like a much longer time. Sonny hadn't even worried about us. From the looks of things, he and Tim had had just about all the ice cream. Well, you have to do something while you watch old summer reruns.

We told Sonny what had happened, and when we boiled it down it really wasn't very much. We still didn't know why Tim's father wanted so bad to get in to see Mr. Peregrine—except that it was something about a will. "Why'd you nudge me when he said that about the will?" I asked Bob. "I couldn't make anything out of it. Did you guess what he was talking about?"

"Only that wills always mean something special when they turn up in mystery stories," Bob said. "Clay has got to be after all that money Mr. Peregrine keeps hidden in his house. If he can't find the money and take it, he'll force Mr. Peregrine to make a will in his favor. Wills are usually why the murder was committed."

"The murder! You think—"

"Not unless we find the corpus delicti," Bob said in a hollow whisper like you read about in books. He knows his hollow whispers make me shiver. "So far we don't even have its bones." He stopped whispering. "Wouldn't it be great, though," he said in his normal excited voice, "if we found a human skeleton to add to my collection? Hey, maybe some of the bones I've got *are* the corpus delicti! I might not be able to tell the difference between cow ribs and human ribs, come to think about it."

"If those things are human," I said, "he sure was a funny-shaped human."

"How do you know it was a he?" Bob said, being shivery again. "Maybe it was a woman—or a girl about eleven-and-a-half years old—"

"Now you're putting me on," I said. "I'm not even going to pretend there's a corpus delicti anywhere."

"You won't have to pretend once I dig it up."

Just then we heard the aunts calling us, and we knew it was bedtime. Well, what *they* thought was bedtime for us. Bedtime is any time we decide to go to sleep, of course, but not many grownups realize that.

Bob told Tim he could watch TV till he got sleepy and then promised to come back and sleep with him after a while. Tim was already sleepy. He sniffled a little, but when Bob patted him, sort of like I do Gibson, he shut up and said, "All wight, Uncle Wobert." At least that's what it sounded like. You can hardly tell what Tim is saying; he's sort of tongue-tied. He might even have been saying he missed his mean old daddy and mama, for all I knew. When I thought about them, I hoped they were getting more and more worried because they couldn't find him. We'd have to be mighty careful that they'd never find him, I knew. They'd really punish him if they got him back before we decided to turn them in to the police.

Bob and I kissed Tim good night, but Sonny

wouldn't. I think he was jealous because Tim liked Bob the best, but Sonny just said it was silly to kiss kids. Maybe it was, but I felt we were doing the right thing to make Tim feel better about what had happened to him all in one day.

When we got upstairs, Aunt Emma said, "Where have you children been? I've been calling you for the longest time."

"Down in the playroom," I said.

Bob added, "Mama lets us watch TV down there till bedtime, Aunt Emma."

"You say you want to watch TV till bedtime? But it's already bedtime," Aunt Emma said. Sonny giggled. I decided to tell him we shouldn't laugh—we might be deaf ourselves sometime. Or Dad might. It might run in the family. Poor Aunt Emma couldn't help it.

She said, "I'm sure your mother said nine o'clock. Is that when you start taking your baths, or are you supposed to have had them by nine?"

"In the summer," I told her, as loud as I could, "we get to play outside till nine, and then we take our baths and go to bed. Bob gets first bath, because he's the oldest. I'm going to use Mama's and Dad's bath tonight and take mine at the same time. Then Sonny can have whichever bath is vacant first. Good night, Aunt Emma. 'Night, Aunt Cammie." I started upstairs to get my night things. Aunt Emma didn't hear it all, but I guess she got the idea. Any other night Sonny would have had to take his bath first, but tonight Bob needed to get through in a hurry, and being oldest is always a good excuse for doing anything he wants to first.

"Good night, children," both aunts said. The boys said good night too and raced up the stairs. I came back down; the master bedroom and bath are downstairs. That's where the aunts slept, of course, but they had decided to stay out on the porch a little longer. They never talked about anything interesting, or I might have eavesdropped. As it was, I hurried to finish my bath and get back upstairs before they wanted some more conversation. It was exhausting, even when you realized it wasn't their fault they couldn't hear too well.

Going back up, I met Bob on the stairs. He was hurrying, too, to get down to the playroom again before the aunts saw him. They'd never check up, of course, after they thought we were safely upstairs.

"Lock the outside door," I whispered. "Clay might have found out who we were and be trying to get us."

"I don't think so," Bob whispered back. "But of course I'll lock it. 'Night, Debbi."

" 'Night."

I could hear Sonny splashing in the tub. It was a nice normal sound, just like I heard every night of my life. There was no reason for me to feel as if something were about to happen—something terrible. But I caught myself shivering, even though it was a hot night.

I was thankful Bob had rescued Tim, of course. But what had he got us into?

Now it was quite dark. I went to the window after I put out the light. I always say my prayers at the window, looking up at the sky, because God's there somewhere. I like to look at the sky when it's like dark blue velvet. Or even when it's got wild black clouds scudding across it like they're chasing one another, or a few stars, or a big fat moon. I just happen to like the sky.

My window is on the side next to Mr. Peregrine's house, and of course when I looked down I could see into his back yard even better than from the oak tree, except much farther away. But this was a dark night, with the moon showing itself from behind the clouds only once in a while. A hide-and-seek sort of night. And there's nothing to see when it's that dark but tree branches and shadows.

Except on this night.

This night there was a small shaft of light in Mr. Peregrine's yard. Light that moved cautiously. Like it was in somebody's hand. Like somebody was around who had no business being there in the dark with a flashlight.

I thought I'd better not tell Sonny; he might get in the way. But I did need Bob if I was going to do anything about it. For a minute I felt like not doing anything about it. I felt like just being a coward and going to bed and not worrying about whether Clay was trying to break into Mr. Peregrine's house or not.

But the chance to find out what Clay wanted with Mr. Peregrine—and how it might matter to what we did about Tim—was too good to pass up. Besides, we are very nosey children. It gets us into lots of trouble, too.

I hurried into my shorts and shirt and sneakers and went very cautiously downstairs. The aunts had gone to bed by now; the front door was locked and the chain was on. I slipped down the basement steps to the playroom door.

But for some silly reason Bob had locked it from the inside. I knocked and knocked, but he didn't come. I called, but not very loud because I didn't want to be heard by anyone but Bob. Then I gave up and hurried to the outside playroom door. No luck there either. The maid's room is at the back of the playroom, without a window, and I realized that at this rate I'd never wake up Bob.

And whoever was fooling around in Mr. Peregrine's yard might get away. I had to watch him. Maybe follow him. And I knew I might have to do it without Bob because it was a right-now thing. I might have to do it by myself.

That was a scary thought. But if I was too scared to ever take any chances, I'd never have any fun. I'd be sitting around playing dolls with girls, instead of going along with Bob and Sonny and Stephen Lee and Benny and the rest of their friends. I usually end up not being cautious at all, even when I know better, just to show them I'm as good as they are.

I gave up on making Bob hear me. I took a deep breath and ran as quietly as I could to the oak tree and shinnied up it. The flashlight's beam was moving toward the side of the yard where my tree's branches

overhung the wall, but I couldn't see who was holding
it, because everything behind a light in the dark is
hard to see. It was moving very slowly, though. It
might be a while before he got to where I could see
him, even if the moon came out. I wondered why he
was moving so slowly. Then I figured it out. He
seemed to be looking for something that might have
been not too easy to find. Something close to the
ground. The light was moving around the way I moved
mine when I was hunting for my ring that night I
missed it and wanted to find it before Mama noticed it
was gone.

There was still time for me to wiggle out on a limb
that stretched over the wall and the old Stanford
burying ground. Maybe that was what he was looking
for! Though it wasn't all that hard to find, I knew.

Very quietly, trying not to make the leaves rustle or
the twigs crackle, I slid along the limb, one leg on
each side of it, inching my way with my hands in
front of me to give the rest of me a lift. It was like
doing push-ups sitting down. The bark was rough on
my bottom, but I didn't let it bother me. Well, not
much. Dad said one time that the secret of getting
along in life is to be able to endure. I didn't know
what he meant then, but I thought I was beginning to
see. He meant that if you can just stick it out, whatever it is, you'll be all right. I was determined to
stick it out.

I heard a slight noise, and it seemed to come from
our yard. I looked down and saw a vague somebody
climbing up my tree. It was too dark to see who it was,

but I wasn't afraid it was anybody who'd hurt me—it had to be Bob. I felt really glad, because Bob is a help most of the time.

I was keeping an eye on the flashlight beam and at the same time trying to see Bob. Whoever was holding the light had stopped and was poking around in Mr. Peregrine's lilacs, which were growing at the heads of some of the graves. Their roots reached right down into the coffins, Bob said. There were a lot of weeds growing around there too, I remembered. Mr. Peregrine never did do any yard work, and Mama said his yard was a good example of survival of the fittest because only the strongest plants could outdo the weeds. But he had some old-fashioned roses that smelled like heaven in the middle of the day. Some hot noontimes I could smell them all the way up in my perch in the tree. The lilacs and day lilies were pretty strong growers, too. And violets. In early spring, before the weeds started to come out, his whole yard was covered with violets. I wondered who planted them.

The flashlight was still wavering around in the lilac bushes when I heard a soft scrambling behind me and knew Bob had got to my limb. I turned to caution him to be very quiet, putting my finger on my lips.

The moon came out for a minute just then, but I still couldn't see very well for the leaves. But Bob is taller than I am and the kid behind me on the limb wasn't.

He inched a little closer, and I made out that it was Sonny.

"Go back!" I whispered violently. "You aren't al-

lowed to climb this high." Well, nobody made that
rule but me, but it's my tree.

Sonny shook his head. He wasn't going back, and
at the moment I couldn't make him. He hitched himself closer to me and pointed toward the light. "Who's
that?" he whispered. The beam had started to move

again, and in our direction, but it was still pointed
toward the ground.

"Might be Tim's father," I whispered back.

As the light got nearer I heard a mutter from its
direction—a very annoyed mutter. "If I could only
see—" Well, you couldn't blame him for wishing the

moon would stay out. I wished it myself—so we could see who he was.

Sonny was practically leaning against me now, and I began to realize why. He was scared and thought for some reason that he'd be safer close to me. I guess that's natural, to want to huddle up with somebody when you're scared. But even though I understood, I thought Sonny was getting too close for comfort. And we were almost too far out on the limb; it was bending a little. I nudged him to get him to go back, but lightly because I didn't want him to holler. And I felt something unusual where his stomach ought to have been, under his shirt front. "What's that?" I whispered, even more violently.

"Only my dynamite," he whispered back. He carried that stuff with him nearly everywhere he went except to Sunday school, and not there only because Mama usually inspected us before we left on Sunday mornings. "I thought we might need it. I saw you slip out, so I grabbed it and came too."

"Sonny, please go back." He shook his head again; he's a very stubborn kid. I didn't dare even whisper after that, because the flashlight was coming very close now.

All at once there was a wild, unearthly screech from where the light showed. And when we jumped from sheer fright, our limb cracked. Loudly.

I could feel it breaking off near the trunk. Sonny clutched me, screaming too.

And then we were falling.

THE SKULL
IN THE BOXWOOD

You don't know what scared is till you've fallen out of a tree late at night into a bunch of broken-down gravestones, practically on top of somebody you think might be a mean guy who beats up his own little kid, and there's an awful scream still ringing in your ears.

My heart was thumping out loud, and Sonny was still yelling, too. He had landed on top of me, so I knew he couldn't be hurt any more than I was, and I found I was able to stand up. I hadn't broken anything. I pulled Sonny up, too, and got us off that weird grave of M.C.'s, which is where we had landed. It was nearly caving in. And then at last I dared to look at that flashlight, which was shining on us now.

My eyes were blinking, but I raised them slowly past the light to the hand that held it, then up the shirt sleeve and on to the shoulder and then to the face. We were close enough to him now to see who it was.

And it wasn't Clay I saw. It was old Mr. Peregrine

himself. He must have lost something, like I did my ring that time, I thought. But why he couldn't have waited till morning to find it, I didn't know.

"What in the world?" Mr. Peregrine said in an astonished voice, putting out his hand as if he had to touch us to see if we were real. Just then I half-saw, half-heard something leap past us, heading toward the wall, and recognized that long-distance leap. It was Gibson. Now that I saw him I realized what the unearthly screech was. Gibson must have been down there under the lilacs and Mr. Peregrine had probably poked him with his cane. Gibson always makes that sound when he's surprised and indignant—for instance, if Aunt Emma accidentally steps on his tail. It sounds worse at night, though, especially when you aren't expecting it.

"Who's that?" Mr. Peregrine said. "Children? Are there two of you? Yes? Where did you come from? In my back field—at night—"

I wanted to ask some questions myself, like what had he lost and could we maybe help him look for it. But I realized he had a right to know what we were doing dropping down in his field in the middle of the night. I didn't know what to tell him, because we were just snooping, of course. And I have heard that trespassing's against the law.

"I'm sorry," I stammered. "And Sonny is too. We live next door. I'm Debbi Howard. We were just climbing up in our tree, and the limb broke—right after Gibson yowled."

"Gibson?" Mr. Peregrine said.

"Our cat. That was what went over the wall just now, if you were wondering, sir."

"It did occur to me to wonder," Mr. Peregrine said mildly. He didn't sound very angry at all. His voice was shaky and sort of slow, the way old people's voices get, but nice. "But a cat named Gibson? I never would have guessed."

"He's really named for a friend of Dad's, Mr. Tom Gibson, who gave him to us when Gib was a kitten," I explained. "But most of Dad's and Mama's friends seem to think he's named after a drink that has a little pickled onion in it. His eyes are green, but sometimes, to people who are having lots of cocktails, they look pale and round and sort of like little onions. I think they're reaching way out, when they say that, though. Mama says they're just making conversation." Then I realized that this was what I was doing too—making conversation—just rattling on because I was nervous and didn't know what to say. Sonny was still crying and not being a bit of help. He wasn't making any conversation, that's for sure.

"Are you hurt, child?" Mr. Peregrine asked him.

"His name's Sonny, sir. At least that's what we call him. His real name is Neil. I don't think he's hurt, just scared. He shouldn't have followed me; the limb wouldn't have broken if there hadn't been two of us on it. I hope we didn't mash your lilacs," I said, feeling as if I ought to apologize. "We didn't mean to do it."

Sonny pulled at my arm. "I want to go home," he wailed. "How will we ever get out?"

"Hush," I told him.

"Why does he think he won't get out?" Mr. Peregrine asked.

"Because your wall is too high for him to climb, sir," I said honestly. "He's tried it. And your iron gate in the wall is always locked with that rusty old lock. And you wouldn't let us go through your house, would you?"

"Why, yes, of course I'll let you come through my house," Mr. Peregrine said. "You don't seem like bad children. You've never bothered me. I'll take you in the back way."

I could hardly believe it. He didn't realize we had been spying on him. He thought we were just climbing the tree in the dark for fun. I felt guilty for deceiving a nice old guy like that. But then, actually we were spying because we thought it was Clay trespassing, and we wanted to help Mr. Peregrine. It didn't seem quite so bad when I figured it out that way.

And we were going to get to see inside Mr. Peregrine's house! I was so excited I almost couldn't stand it. Bob would die when he heard what an adventure he'd missed.

We crossed the field—slowly, because Mr. Peregrine didn't walk very fast—and then went across the back yard, which was just as weedy as the field behind it.

The back door to the latticed porch wasn't locked, and he didn't lock it after us. I couldn't help wondering if Mr. Peregrine always left it unlocked. Of course he had no idea anybody was trying to get in, and the

locked gate and the high wall would seem like more
than enough protection in a nice little town like ours.
I wished I could warn him about Clay, but things
would get too complicated if I tried to warn him without giving away how I knew Clay's plans.

I did say, though, "Maybe you ought to lock your
doors, Mr. Peregrine. Sometimes there are robbers
looting people's houses."

"I wouldn't think they'd consider mine a likely pros-
pect." Mr. Peregrine had a funny, rusty-sounding
laugh. I guess he didn't get to use it very much. He
probably didn't realize everybody talked about all the

money hidden in his house. "Does your mother keep all her doors locked all the time?"

"Well, no, sir," I had to admit. "We're pretty careless about it sometimes. We do put on the chains at night, though, when we think about it."

"Well, I always lock my front door," Mr. Peregrine assured us. "And the back gate."

"Is this your back porch, sir?" Sonny said. He had stopped crying and was being his usual curious self. It was a big porch, dark now, with a wooden lattice, and honeysuckle vines growing all over it. I could smell the blooms. They smell sweeter in the dark. "It's not much like ours," Sonny went on. "I never saw a porch like this before."

"I like it," I said, in case Sonny had hurt his feelings.

"Yes, it's a good porch," Mr. Peregrine answered. "We used to eat out here in summer when"—he stopped—"a long time ago."

"It must have been fun to eat on the porch," I said. "Did you have any children then, Mr. Peregrine?"

He didn't answer for a minute. Then he said, "Yes. I had one daughter then. My only child."

"What was her name?" Sonny said.

Mr. Peregrine waited so long to answer this time that it almost seemed as if he couldn't remember and had to stop and think what her name was. Then he said, "It was Rose. Rose Antoinette Peregrine."

"Did she ever get married?" Sonny said. "Do you have any grandchildren like us, Mr. Peregrine?"

"No. She never got married."

He sounded so sad that I thought we'd better not ask any more questions about Rose. She was probably dead, or she'd come to see him sometimes, at least on Father's Day. Somehow it seemed as if it must have been a very long time ago that Mr. and Mrs. Peregrine and Rose ate supper on the back porch with the honeysuckle vines smelling as sweet as they still did. Mrs. Peregrine must have died a long time ago too, I thought, without any reason for thinking so except that everything looked awfully unhousekept. As if it had been years since anybody cared.

He took us into the kitchen, which was no more cleaned up than the porch. Mr. Peregrine sure didn't bother much about picking up after himself. There was one cup and saucer and plate in the sink, and they looked mighty lonely. Seeing them made me sorry for him. I promised myself I'd tell Mama, and she'd probably ask him over to Sunday dinner sometimes. He could be company for the aunts when they visited; maybe they were about the same age. Probably they remembered the same wars, I was thinking. Maybe they even knew each other, back when Mr. Peregrine went out more often.

Mr. Peregrine said, in an old-fashioned way and kind of helplessly, "I'd like to offer you some refreshments, but I can't think of anything I have that you might like. I don't even have any lemons to make lemonade. I drink tea and coffee myself. I don't suppose you children drink anything but milk, do you, Debbi?"

I was surprised that he remembered my name,

when he had had trouble with his own daughter Rose's. "Yes, sir, we drink lots of other things," I said. "Sometimes we have tea too. But we can't stay, thank you. We ought to be in bed, you see. We have to hurry home, before the aunts find out we aren't there."

He couldn't help looking relieved that we couldn't stay. He opened the door to the dining room, and we followed him through. All the ceilings were a mile high, and all the windows had long dark draperies. There was a big old dining-room table with carved legs and carved chairs around it, and a china cupboard with lots of nice china showing through the glass, but it didn't look as if anybody had used it for a long time. There were actually cobwebs hanging in the corners of the room.

The living room was just the same. Cobwebs, lots of dusty furniture with decorative carving, and fascinating knickknacks that I'd have loved to look at if there had been time. A bookcase-desk with carving on the front had the desk part closed up, but the bookshelves had glass over them and all sorts of things inside as well as books—china figurines, girls with lambs, glass paperweights with flowers inside them, a small box with seashells all over it. We went on through to the hall, which was very gloomy too. Mr. Peregrine turned on the lights as we came into each room, but they were dim lights and didn't help much. It was spooky —as if nobody really lived there, not even Mr. Peregrine. He was too solid to be a ghost though.

The hall was like two big long rooms together, with a staircase leading to the upstairs. At one end of the hall was a piano, a big old heavy dark one, another bookcase, and a chair that was so carved with lions and dragons and things it looked like a throne. All the furniture was made of that dark wood that's almost black. Sonny couldn't help asking about the pictures of ships, hanging in heavy frames on the wall. He had never seen any like them before. I hadn't either. "What kind of pictures are they, sir?"

"Why, they're engravings," Mr. Peregrine said. "I have a book here somewhere with lots of pictures like that in it. Would you like to see it?"

"Yes, sir," Sonny said, minding his manners, I was glad to see. Mr. Peregrine started hunting for it in the bookcase, puttering around until I got impatient.

"Maybe that's it, sir," I said, showing him one that was right in front of him, a great big old book.

"Might be," he murmured. When he opened it I could see the kind of pictures he had called engravings, all right, but they weren't of ships; they were of people and angels. The book was *Paradise Lost*, and on the title page it said the illustrations were by Gustave Doré. It looked like the kind of book that would belong to a preacher—or somebody who had once been a preacher.

"Was it *Paradise Lost* you were going to show us?" I asked Mr. Peregrine. "It doesn't have ships in it, but the engravings do look interesting." They didn't really, only old, but I wanted to be polite because he was trying to please us.

"Why don't you take it home with you?" Mr. Peregrine said. "Nobody's looked at it since Rose—"

"Did she like it?" Sonny asked as if he wondered how she could.

"She called it her book when she was small, and she used to look at the pictures before she could read. Even after she grew up, she still liked to look at it sometimes."

"We'll be very careful with it," I promised, "and we'll bring it back, sir. Mama says there's nothing worse than not returning somebody else's books when you borrow them."

"An admirable viewpoint," Mr. Peregrine said. "When you come to bring it back, maybe I'll have some lemonade and animal crackers or something like that."

I didn't tell him we were too old for animal crackers; we like chocolate chips better. "Thank you, sir," I said, taking the big old book carefully. It was dusty, but I didn't wipe it off in case that might hurt his feelings. "Could we," I asked, daring because he was so nice and because I thought he must really want company or he wouldn't have bothered to say that about the lemonade, "bring our brother Bob too? He'd like to meet you."

"I'm sure I'd like to know Bob," Mr. Peregrine said courteously, opening the front door for us. "Tell your mother all three of you are invited."

"Thanks, and good night, sir," I said, and Sonny for a wonder said, "Good night, sir," too, without prompting.

"Good night."

He closed the door, and I hoped he'd lock it. It

was an enormous house, and we hadn't even seen inside all those rooms on the other side of the hall or upstairs. If somebody should get in who didn't belong there, I thought, he could hide anywhere and Mr. Peregrine might not even know he was there. Probably Mr. Peregrine slept in one of the downstairs bedrooms that must be on the other side of the hall, and he might not ever go upstairs at all. He might not know who was living up there! I shivered at the idea. Suppose you thought you were alone in a spooky house like that and there was really a man like Clay hiding and watching you?

Sonny said, "What did you let him lend us that old book for? I don't want to look at it."

"I don't either, but we had to be polite. You were the one who talked about the pictures. But I think poor Mr. Peregrine's lonesome, and he lent it to us so we'd have to come back to see him to return it. We'll just keep it a while so he'll think we're reading it and then take it back. And wait till we tell Bob! At first we'll let him think we're the only ones invited back—bug him a while before we let on that he can come too."

"Yeah. That'll bug Bob all right."

"Did you leave the latch off, Sonny, so we could get back in without waking anybody up?"

" 'Course. You think I'm stupid or something?"

We were at the back door. There's a big old clump of boxwood bushes right by the steps. They were black and shadowy in the grayness. I had never even

thought about anybody's hiding there. But as I put my foot on the bottom step, I heard something that petrified me.

It was a weird whisper coming out of that mess of boxwood. "I——see——you——" Then there was a sound like chains clanking, and I could dimly make out a white thing among the green-black leaves. "I——see——you——"

Sonny clutched me, and I'm not ashamed to admit I clutched him back. We were even too scared to run.

Just then the moon came out from behind those heavy clouds. The moonlight lit up the white thing that showed in the middle of the boxwood.

We could see what it was now.

But it couldn't be. It looked like a human skull!

And it made a sudden move toward us.

THE BAD GUYS MOVE IN

My throat was too dry to scream, but Sonny's wasn't. We both fell back off the step and tangled on the ground, with my brain telling me I had to shush Sonny before he woke a lot of people up, and at the same time my legs frantically telling me we had to get away from that terrifying thing in the boxwood.

I put my hand over Sonny's mouth, and yanked him up with the other hand. "Come on," I managed to say. "We've got to run—before it touches us—" All I could think of was that I'd die if it touched me.

Just as we started to run I heard another sepulchral whisper, "You——can't——get——away——"

I stopped dead still, disgusted with myself for being scared because now I recognized that hollow whisper. "Shut up, Sonny," I said, taking my hand off his mouth. "It's only Bob, trying to scare us."

Bob came out from behind the boxwood, laughing all over, clanking the chain he locks his bicycle with. "Trying to! You should've seen how you looked! I never saw anybody so scared."

"I don't think it's so funny," I told him. "You nearly made Sonny wake up the whole neighborhood."

"If they didn't wake up when you fell out of that tree," Bob said, "they won't now."

"How'd you know we fell out of the tree?" I remembered then all the exciting things we had to tell Bob.

"I know everything," Bob said, maddeningly mysterious. I almost decided not to tell him. He couldn't know everything we knew.

"How did you—?"

"I woke up and couldn't go back to sleep. I don't know what woke me—"

"I tried to," I said.

"It was probably a delayed reaction," Bob surmised. "Tim was asleep, so I went up to see you, Debbi, and you were gone. I looked out your window and when the moon came out I saw somebody running toward the oak tree and guessed it was you. Then I saw the light moving around in Mr. Peregrine's back field and realized you had probably seen it too and were trying to find out what it was. About that time the moon came out again and I saw Sonny sneak across to the tree and start climbing after you. I decided to watch from the window in case you two got caught—I thought you might need somebody to rescue you. But when you went into the house with the one who had the flashlight without trying to get away, I realized it must be Mr. Peregrine and you weren't afraid of him."

"Didn't you wish you were with us?" Sonny said. "We got to see Mr. Peregrine's house!"

"Well, yes," Bob admitted honestly. "I did wish I were there too. But then I decided maybe it was better for me to be on the outside, in case you should be held captive or something."

"He was nice," I said. "He didn't even wonder why we were out so late—maybe he doesn't remember what time children are sent to bed. He lent us this book, and he invited Sonny and me back soon to have lemonade and animal crackers."

"You're too old for animal crackers."

"But we'd be willing to eat some anyway—wouldn't we, Sonny?—to find out if Clay is hiding in one of those rooms we didn't get into tonight. We'd like to solve the mystery, wouldn't we, of what Mr. Peregrine's got that Tim's father wants? Money, of course, but we're curious about the whole thing. So Sonny and I are going back. You don't have to come."

"Oh, I'll come," Bob said hastily.

Sonny nudged me and said, "But, Bob, don't you have to wait for Mr. Peregrine to invite you?"

After a minute Bob said, "Well, I guess so."

He sounded so disappointed that I had to tell him. "It's O.K. We asked if you could come too, and he said yes, he'd like to meet you. So you can come—if you'll pretend you like animal crackers."

"O.K." Bob cheered up.

All this time he was holding that thing in his hand.

"Where'd you get that?"

"Oh, isn't it weird? It'll be the best thing in my collection. You sure were scared."

"Where did it come from?"

"Over there." He nodded toward Mr. Peregrine's. "After you all went into the house, I decided to investigate where the light had been. I got my flashlight and climbed the tree and slid down the limb you broke—it's still hanging—and fished around in the graveyard bushes with my light. All at once I saw the edge of this good old skull. If you two hadn't fallen on top of Mr. Peregrine, he'd surely have seen it in another minute. I'm glad he didn't, because he might have had a heart attack. Seeing something unexpected and awful can sometimes give old people heart attacks. Remember Stephen Lee's grandfather had one when Stephen was bleeding that time the car hit him?"

"Forget Stephen Lee," I said, wishing I'd looked at the ground instead of being so busy trying to find out who held the flashlight. "Go on about the skull!"

"Well, of course I never would have dug into a grave, not even if it had been a hundred-year-old one, not even for a prize for my collection. But most of the dirt on top of this one must have washed off in all these hard rains and thunderstorms we've been having. It wasn't buried so very deep, not six feet under like you read about. Or maybe the grave's sunk in. But I think somebody might have been digging for it a little bit; there was fresh dirt scratched up—"

"Gibson!" Sonny and I said together.

"That's what Gibson was doing there when Mr. Peregrine poked him," Sonny explained to himself.

Bob and I were already way ahead of him.

"Cats are so neat," Sonny went on, "they dig a hole before they—"

73

"Never mind," Bob said. "He hadn't done anything yet, anyhow. I grabbed the skull and shinnied back up the hanging tree limb and over the wall. Then I thought I'd hide and scare you. Tim was sound asleep, so I knew he wouldn't wake up before I got back to him."

"But, Bob," I said slowly, "it's got to be—somebody's—what used to be somebody's—head. Whose?"

"It was in the grave marked *M.C.* But it's nothing but dried bone," Bob said. "So clean it feels like it was made of plastic. It might have belonged to a doctor or a medical school; it's like those. Maybe M.C. was some medical college's skeleton to study anatomy with. You can't feel sorry for it 'specially. I mean, it couldn't have been anybody recent. Not really a corpus delicti. It's

as dry as my cow bones. It doesn't even smell a bit, see?" He thrust it toward me and I jumped back. I don't like dead bones much, even if they aren't a corpus delicti.

"Bob, I think you have to give it to the authorities," I said. "After all, the marker said 'God Will Judge.' And there might be some Stanfords somewhere who'd care. I don't think you can keep it for your collection. No matter how old it is, it was—somebody—once. It has to be buried again—a Christian burial."

"You're probably right," Bob said. "Only the authorities won't know anything about old M.C. if I don't tell them. The Stanfords are all dead; they don't care any more. Lord Byron made a drinking cup out of a skull he found!"

"The monks that used to live at Newstead Abbey haunted the place, too, till somebody gave that drinking cup a Christian burial," I pointed out. I had heard the story too—Aunt Dora told it to us when she came back from her vacation in England.

"Well, if I told anybody," Bob said, "I'd get in trouble for finding it, because it's none of my business. Anyhow, I don't want anybody to know. I might dig there again, the first chance I get, and find the rest of the skeleton. I might decide to tell the authorities later—and then again I might not. I might just decide to solve for myself the mystery of who this good old skull belonged to. If he had a coffin, it's already rotted. But maybe there are clothes that haven't decayed yet, like a belt buckle. Or the family jewels might have been buried with him or—"

"You'll get in trouble," I warned him. But after warning him, I didn't have to tell on him; I had done my duty. And he was right; the authorities really wouldn't know unless we told them.

"Why don't you go on and dig the rest of it up right now?" Sonny challenged. He does like to needle Bob.

But Bob must have had enough for one night, and I didn't encourage any more digging. I don't think he ought to dig in graveyards, even family burying grounds from a long time ago. I'd help him do 'most anything else, but not that. I don't want M.C.'s ghost after me.

Bob answered Sonny, "Because I don't want to right now. I have to get back in case Tim wakes up and gets scared. And I have to find a good place to hide the skull. Somewhere in the playroom where nobody will see it."

"Just put it with all your other bones, down under the cow ribs or somewhere like that," I suggested. "I don't think anybody would find it there. Mama wouldn't go shoving those bones around for anything. And another bone or two won't make much difference in how the collection looks to the meter-reading man."

"Good idea," he said. "I thought of the same thing. Let's go do it now. Come on."

We went through the playroom door, instead of the house back door, and Bob locked it on the inside. We glanced in at Tim, sleeping peacefully with his mouth open—he must have had adenoids—and his dirty old toy rabbit hugged in his arm. Its name was George, as near as we could make out what he was saying.

Then we helped Bob hide the skull, and I made him wash his hands over and over, like a doctor. I washed mine, too, even though I hadn't touched the skull. You feel like you ought to, somehow, when you get near a thing like that. I don't think bones are so great for a collection, and I often wished Bob liked to collect coins or stamps instead.

We had to stay up a little while longer to tell Bob about Mr. Peregrine's house and his daughter Rose Antoinette. He was very interested and thought we ought to go back the next day, but I knew that was too soon. Nobody would read that book in one day, even if he could. And we had too many other things to do to even start reading it right away.

"What about the mystery?" I said. "I wish we could find out who was buried under Mr. Peregrine's lilacs. As well as who buried him. Without digging up any more of him, of course."

"Maybe it wasn't a him," Bob said. "Maybe it was a woman. You can't tell from the skull."

"Can you tell from the rest of it?"

"I don't think I can," Bob said candidly, "but doctors and scientists can. I'll be able to after I go to college and study archaeology and maybe anatomy and osteology."

"You plan to wait that long to solve the mystery?"

" 'Course not. Next time Mr. Peregrine goes out— like when we see him heading down toward the shopping center—we'll go over there and dig up the rest of the skeleton. Nobody can see us behind that wall. We may not know, though, if it's a man or a woman till I decide to tell somebody and then let them investigate. Probably the historical society would like to know who M.C. was and why God will judge him."

"I think you ought to tell them now," Sonny said. "It might be important. And they can put you in jail for finding it and not telling them."

"No," Bob said cheerfully. "I'm not old enough for jail yet."

"I'm not helping you dig up any graves," I said, "and neither is Sonny. Come on, Sonny. We'd better go up the inside steps and let Bob lock the top door behind us."

In the morning Bob kept watching for Mr. Peregrine to go to the store, but he never came out of his house. It was a good thing we were still watching, though, or we might not have seen Clay and Adele come that evening after supper.

They drove up in that old car of theirs, and he left her in it while he went to the door. I threw the ball we were playing with down in front of the house so Sonny could chase it and see what happened. He came back and said, "The door opened and they talked a minute and then Clay went inside."

"Mr. Peregrine shouldn't have let him in." I was worried. "That's where he made his big mistake. He's going to be sorry—"

Sonny said, "Why are we bothering? After all—"

"Because of Tim," I said, and Bob added, "If we could get something else on Clay, Tim wouldn't have to go back to him even if the police did find out where

Tim is. It's pretty clear that Clay is trying to put something over on Mr. Peregrine, and whatever it is, it's probably a crime. We like Mr. Peregrine and Tim, and we don't like Clay and Adele. So we're keeping an eye on them, that's all."

"Well, I'm tired of keeping an eye over there," Sonny said. "I'm going to watch TV with Tim. O.K.?"

"Right. You stay with Tim," Bob said. "And put some more of that Mercurochrome on his cuts."

"All right. But he hollers unless you do it." Sonny left.

"Look!" Bob said. "Clay's coming back to the car. And Adele's getting out."

I said, "And—Bob—suitcases! They brought their things, like they're going to stay with Mr. Peregrine."

"I'm pretty sure he doesn't want to have company," Bob said. "He never would. But they're moving right in on him."

"How can they?" I said indignantly. "He could call the police to put them out."

"They're stronger than he is. And," Bob said slowly, "he might not want the police snooping around, for some reason."

I got it. "You mean because of the newer grave in the family graveyard, you think Mr. Peregrine's afraid of the police?" After all, he did build that high wall and always kept the gate locked.

"I don't know. But you don't just let the bad guys move in on you without any reason. Just because they're stronger and could overpower you. Of course, he doesn't have a telephone, does he?"

"I guess not. No wires. What if they've already over-powered him?" I said, and I was sort of scared. "Maybe he's tied up in there, or killed—"

"No, they want him to sign a will before he dies. Well," Bob said, and he put on his reckless look, "we can't call the police because we don't want to get Mr. Peregrine in trouble. And they'd just say it was none of our business. But we can't just stand by and do nothing while the people who beat Tim get in there and do something awful to Mr. Peregrine."

I tried to look reckless too, but I can't do it as well as Bob. "What else can we do? We're just kids."

"Well," Bob said, and he narrowed his eyes and looked very determined, "we can't keep them from moving in on Mr. Peregrine. But maybe we can make them move out."

"How?"

"It's a spooky-looking old house, especially at night. With lots of empty rooms. And the back door stays un-locked, you found out. Debbi, how would you like to be a ghost?"

TWO GHOSTS
IN THE SECRET ROOM

"We'd never dare," I said. "Would we?"

There was nothing to it, except for persuading Sonny to stay with Tim. That was what was hard. We bribed him, though: Bob gave him a dime and I promised not to tell what he'd done when Mama and Dad got back. I didn't really know of anything wrong he'd done, but there was bound to be something he'd rather not have mentioned. He knew what it was even if I didn't.

We spent the time until dark in the playroom fixing up the skull with luminous paint from Bob's bike kit— he had been painting the bike in places to make it safer to ride at night, even though so far he'd not been allowed to ride it at night. He wanted it to be ready in case of an emergency. In an emergency the ordinary rules wouldn't count, he figured. I've noticed if a person's a hero, nobody says anything about the safety rules he broke while he was saving somebody's life or something.

There was enough of the quick-drying paint left from the bike to go around the skull's eye sockets and the nose hollow and to cover the teeth and outline the head. Bob did it; I wouldn't touch it. "It's going to look very spooky," he said with satisfaction. "Let's cover it up, though, till we get ready for Clay and Adele to see it." We wrapped it in an old towel, the inside of which Bob had smeared with the rest of the paint so as to have something else to give off a ghostly light.

"Let's skip the chain," Bob said. "It's not really heavy enough to sound very much like Marley's ghost, anyhow. And it might rattle at the wrong time."

"O.K. Is it dark enough now?"

"Turn off the set, Sonny, and the light. You can have it back in a minute."

Tim started to cry and holler "Uncle Wobert!" when Sonny blacked out the TV, so Bob said, "Well, turn it back on. We'll go in the maid's room to try this out. Better that way anyhow; it would probably scare Tim. Sonny, you want to be scared?"

"I want to see it," Sonny said. "I'm not scared."

"Come on."

We shut the door and the maid's room was pitch-black. Slowly Bob uncovered the skull and turned it toward us. It was really horrible! I almost screamed myself, even though I was expecting it. And the towel had just enough of the glow stuff on it to glimmer faintly, like maybe a glob of ectoplasm.

"That's pretty good," Sonny admitted, and Bob said happily, "It sure is. Here, you hold it so I can see it from a distance."

Sonny didn't mind holding the thing, and Bob looked at it from all angles. "It's O.K. Bound to scare Clay and Adele. Come on, Debbi. We've got to convince the aunts we've gone upstairs to bed. You'd better come too, Sonny, and say good night to them, and then sneak back down in a few minutes." He wrapped up the skull again and we went back to Tim. "You and George be good and watch TV till Sonny gets back," Bob told him.

"O.K., Uncle Wobert." Tim held out that old rabbit to Bob and Bob patted it. Tim was happy with a peppermint stick Bob had brought him. He had brought one for George too and told Tim to eat George's himself if George didn't finish it. I think Bob makes a pretty nice uncle for a little kid to have. Mickey is going to like her Uncle Robert, if she ever gets to see him. When Dad and Mama had called before supper, they'd said they didn't think Betsy and Mickey could come back home with them because Mickey was still in the incubator, being premature and very small, and besides Joe would miss them too much while he was in the hospital recuperating. So Dad and Mama were staying a couple more days if everything at home was all right. We said everything was fine.

Of course when we said good night to the aunts, Aunt Cammie got curious about what Bob was doing with that towel rolled up under his arm. He said he'd been painting and got some paint on it, which was true. "I'll put it in the wash when I get through, Aunt Cammie," he said.

"Wash your shoe?" Aunt Cammie said. "You mustn't use the towels on your shoes, Bob. Don't you know your mother wouldn't like that?"

"Yes, ma'am," Bob said as loud as he could. "All right, I won't wash my shoes with it, I promise, Aunt Cammie."

We escaped upstairs to wait in Bob's room till they went into the downstairs bedroom. "We have to put on black clothes," Bob said, "so we won't show in the dark. All that's supposed to show up is the ghost."

"We haven't got any black clothes."

"Well, maybe our jeans are dark enough, and we could wear those dark blue knit shirts with the long sleeves that we had last winter."

"They'll be awfully hot."

"We can stand it."

"What about our faces?"

"I guess we'll just have to black our faces," Bob said.

"With what?" I didn't much want to.

Bob looked around. There wasn't a thing black in his room.

Sonny said, "The fireplace in the living room—there's soot on the back of it. I got some on my hands once and it was real black. And hard to wash off," he added.

"And what were you doing in the fireplace?" I said sternly.

"Nothing! Just creeping around. Anyhow, you promised not to tell, Debbi."

"Well, maybe I won't, if you go on back down there

in the playroom with Tim now. See if the coast is clear, first." I guess I never will know what Sonny was doing in the fireplace, since I was supposed to know already.

He reported that the downstairs bedroom door was shut and went back to baby-sit Tim.

When Bob and I were dressed in the dark clothes, and he had covered the towel bundle with another dark shirt, we slipped down to the living room. Even if it was Sonny's idea, the soot was pretty neat. We blacked each other's faces and necks and the backs of our hands and the tops of our bare feet. Nothing showed white but our eyes and teeth. We left the back door unlocked as we went out. I carried the flashlight, because Bob would handle the skull.

The dangling tree limb was still good for getting down into Mr. Peregrine's field. Everything was dark and nothing moved. Since I had been in the house before and knew the lay of the land, Bob said I should lead the way.

"I hope I can remember the lay of the land," I answered doubtfully.

At least the back door was easy; it was still unlatched.

The hall was dark. But way down at the other end a streak of light showed under a closed door. "They must be down there," I whispered.

"Let's explore the upstairs," Bob said. I never would have dared, without him, but two can do more dangerous things than one.

"Suppose one of them's up there?"

"It's a chance we have to take."

Now we were in new territory, where I didn't know the lay of the land at all. But an upstairs is usually full of bedrooms. Since no light showed under any of the doors, we guessed nobody was around. "Walk very softly and don't drop anything," Bob whispered. "You know how loud overhead noises sound when you're downstairs. I'm glad we came barefooted."

"They aren't right under this room, though," I said, cautiously opening a door. "And in a house like this, they'd blame any noises on ghosts." It was dark inside the room, of course, until I flashed my light around. Nothing was there but the usual bedroom furniture, but the whole thing looked old and dusty and un-lived-in. We looked in both the other rooms on the same side of the hall. They were just like the first, cobwebby and dusty. One of them had a lot of junk in it, like somebody's mixed-up attic.

"Let's look on the other side and see if there's any way out of the other rooms in case our ghost has to make a fast getaway," Bob said.

There were two doors. We found nothing mysterious at first, only another bedroom, but I guessed it was the room Adele and Clay meant to sleep in. It looked just as weird as the others, but it had suitcases on the chairs and the window had been opened. I wanted to see what those two had in the suitcases, but Bob said there wasn't time; we might get caught and we hadn't made a plan of action yet or found a way to get out.

That room had a door leading into a very old-look-ing bathroom that had wallpaper instead of tiles and a claw-footed tub and a tank hanging over the toilet with a chain to pull for flushing. I wished Mama could have seen it. She likes antiques, and I bet she never saw an antique toilet at an auction.

I saw Bob looking puzzled.

"What's the matter?"

"Debbi," he said slowly, "there's something very strange about this. Doesn't it strike you that there ought to be a door to the other bedroom from in here? When the bathroom's between two rooms, there's usually a door to both of them. Here's a door to the hall and of course one to this bedroom, but not one to the other bedroom."

"Which other bedroom?" I said. "There isn't any other on this side of the hall. Only two doors, remember? This bathroom door and the bedroom door we came in by. There were three on the other side, but—"

"You're right! But there's space for another big room. This bathroom and the one bedroom we came through can't possibly take up all the space on this side of the hall, which matches the three rooms on the other side. So is it a secret room? A room with no door?" He took the flashlight and looked over the bathroom wallpaper. "I can't see well enough to tell if a door's been boarded up," he said disappointedly. He slipped into the hall and looked at that wall too. "More wallpaper," he reported. "Could be a door behind it, I guess, if somebody filled in the space before papering."

"It can't be a really secret room, though, because anybody can see it ought to be here," I said.

"I wonder," Bob said. "Come here, Debbi." Flashing the light ahead of us, I followed him back to the bedroom. "I thought I remembered," he said excitedly. "See, there's a kind of balcony on this side. I think that long window is what they call a French window, to take the place of a door in going out to the little balcony. Good thing they left it open." He stuck his head out. "Sure enough, the balcony goes past another window farther along!"

"The window to the secret room!" I said.

"We've just got to go and look into it," Bob said. "There's a big old tree by that end, with a limb we could reach to climb down if we get cut off from inside the house."

I agreed. I couldn't have stood it not to see into the secret room. But the balcony did look mighty rickety. "Are you sure we ought to risk this balcony? Suppose it breaks like my tree limb did?"

"It won't break," Bob said confidently. "And anyway, hold onto the side of the house."

There wasn't anything to hold on to, just smooth boards. But we were lucky and the balcony, shaky though it seemed, held our weight.

We inched along in the dark to the other window, which turned out to be a French window too. There were curtains over it, and the glass was so dirty we couldn't see inside the room at all, even when I flashed the light in.

"See if you can open it," I urged. "Let's get inside!"

But Bob was the one getting cautious now. "I guess we don't have any right to break into a room Mr.

Peregrine sure doesn't seem to want anybody to go into," he said reluctantly, "even if we are here trying to help him get rid of Clay and Adele. Maybe it would be all right to just look in, though, if I could get the French window open."

He turned the knob, and it moved. Everything was so quiet, I was afraid the rusty screak could be heard.

Just as he was about to pull open the long window, though, we heard another noise besides the screak—a strange sound inside the house. It took us a minute to realize what it was. That antique toilet sure made a lot of noise when it was flushed.

"They've come upstairs!" I whispered to Bob. He nodded, motioning me to follow him back along the balcony to the window of the room they were in, pointing to the wrapped-up thing under his arm.

To be honest, right then I'd rather have explored the secret room than scared Clay and Adele. But that was our excuse for being here. I went along.

Not making a bit of noise, we crept to the side of the open window, where the draperies would keep us from being seen. I was glad there were plenty of clouds over the moon. It was so dark I could hardly see Bob. But the light inside the room, though it was dim like the rest of Mr. Peregrine's light bulbs, showed us Adele, looking for something in her suitcase, grumbling to herself about how the old man was trying to save on electricity when he had all that money.

"Clay's still in the bathroom," Bob whispered. "Now's the time to give her a scare!"

He unwrapped the skull. It glimmered in the dark,

frighteningly. He held it just outside the window, where it would show up against the black of the night and not be touched by the room's faint light.

I stood, petrified, watching Adele while he made a *woooo—ooo-ooo* sound like a sick banshee. She turned her head, startled.

"Go a——wa——ay," Bob moaned. "Go a——wa ——ay from this house—" He moved the towel slightly, and then waved the skull a bit toward the window.

Adele shrieked. I never heard such a scream. She was scared all right. I had been thinking maybe we were silly to try to scare them away, but if it had been only Adele we could have done it. She must have been the superstitious type; she scared easy.

I was glad Bob had the sense to let well enough alone for once. He whipped the dark shirt over the skull to hide it, and started running as fast as he could along the balcony, not even thinking now about whether the wood was rotten. I was right behind him. We could hear Adele screaming for Clay to come quick.

"We can't make it down that tree before he comes!" I panted. "Oh, Bob, what'll we do? He'll catch us, for sure!"

THE CLUE
IN THE OLD BOOK

We heard Clay's voice at the other window hollering at Adele, and we heard her saying hysterically, "It was right out there—a ghost telling us to get out of this house. Clay, I don't want to stay here another minute!"

"Don't be a fool!" he said roughly. "Let me look—"

Bob hesitated. I nearly bumped into him before I could stop running. I knew in a split second what he was going to do, before he did it—it was like Fate. I had to follow him; there was nothing else to do if we weren't to be caught.

Bob hurriedly opened the French window into the secret room, and we slipped inside and shut it again. "Stand to the side of the window," Bob whispered. "Then if he opens it from outside, at least he won't see us unless he really searches the room."

Luck was with us. Clay didn't even open that window. We could hear him grumbling at Adele, "There's nothing out here at all. You're imagining things, Adele. And you've got me risking my life on a rotten balcony that wouldn't even hold up a ghost if one did climb up this high."

After a few minutes that seemed an awful lot longer, I whispered, "He's not coming after us, Bob. Do we dare turn on the flashlight and see what the room looks like?"

"O.K. I wonder why the doors into here—if there were doors—were covered up."

I flashed the light around. This room, too, had cobwebs and dust. But it was different from the other bedrooms. They all had dark heavy furniture and draperies that looked like winter was there all year long. This room looked like summer—at least it would have if it had been dusted and the sun were shining in. The furniture was white with gold trimmings, and the wallpaper had pink rosebuds twining up pale green arbors. The rugs were green, and the bed had four posts and a canopy made of white organdy with pink roses, like the counterpane. The window curtains were white organdy, too. And there was a closed door in the hall side of the wall that could've been covered up on the other side.

Bob said, "Wow! What—?"

I knew. "It's—it's got to be Rose's room, Bob. Don't you see? All the rose stuff? Her mother must have liked roses. And when she had a baby girl she named her Rose. And fixed up her room with roses. All that long time ago."

"You must be right," Bob said. "But Rose must have done something awful for Mr. Peregrine to have closed up her room like it never was here."

"Maybe she only died," I surmised. "Sometimes when a person dies the mother or somebody wants to leave her room just like it was on the last day of her life and locks it up so it won't ever be disturbed. I've read about cases like that."

"But whoever would do that is out of her mind," Bob said.

I shivered. Maybe Mr. Peregrine was—?

"Besides," Bob said, "the door wasn't just locked. It was erased. Wiped out." His whisper sounded eerie there in Rose's ghostly room. I knew he was thinking about the skull he had found in the yard—the thing he was still holding wrapped up under his arm.

"It couldn't be," I said faintly. "Mr. Peregrine couldn't have."

"Well, I hope not," Bob said. "He doesn't look like a Jack the Ripper to me. Besides, her initials weren't M.C."

"Maybe they were for 'My Child'?" I shivered when the idea struck me. "Maybe he—but he couldn't. He was a preacher. What are we going to do now?"

"Get out of here. I think we've scared Adele enough for one night. She wants to leave already."

We tiptoed to the French window, and Bob stuck his head out and looked toward the other window. "It's safe," he whispered. "Come on."

I knew the balcony wasn't as shaky as it looked, since it had held Clay. But still I found myself walking light, as if it might fall if I put my whole weight down on it. "Hurry," Bob said, and we made it to the other end and saw thankfully that the tree limb touching

the rail was sturdy. In fact, that might have been what
was holding up the balcony.

Bob threw his leg over the rail, and caught the tree
limb with one hand, still hanging onto the skull with
the other. I warned, "You watch yourself!" I climbed
over cautiously and hung onto the tree. I was used to
climbing around in my oak tree, so it wasn't any problem to slide down this one.

At the foot Bob said, "Are you O.K.?" and I said, "Sure."

"Let's go home," he said. We slipped like black ghosts through the field and over to our tree, where the broken limb was waiting like a faithful ladder for us to climb getting over the wall. As we looked back at Mr. Peregrine's house, there was a light visible in what we supposed was the downstairs front bedroom, probably his room. We guessed he was going to bed. But the rooms with the balcony were on the other side of the house, so we couldn't see their windows.

"Poor Mr. Peregrine," I said. "He must be hating them for being there, and if he can't get rid of them without—"

"Without telling everybody what he's hiding," Bob said.

"They might be there from now on," I said. "So we don't dare let Tim show his nose outside, ever." We had been wondering, before this, if we couldn't let Tim play in the back yard sometimes when the aunts were taking their naps. But now that wouldn't do.

In the playroom Tim was fast asleep, George too, but Sonny was waiting to hear what had happened. He said the late show wasn't too good.

While we tried to get the soot off our faces, we told him all we'd done. It wasn't easy to get that stuff off. When Bob looked at the soot we had smeared around the maid's bathroom, he said, "Think of the finger-prints we left!"

"If Adele sees them on her door, maybe she'll think

the ghost left them," I said, and giggled. Adele wasn't very bright, I had already figured, since two kids like us could scare her with that Halloween sort of stuff. I was cleaning up the bathroom, because of course we didn't want to leave clues to link us to anything.

"Well," Bob said as Sonny and I started to sneak upstairs to bed, "if it were only Adele, they might be out of there tomorrow. But I don't think Clay is as easy to scare as she is."

He was right; Clay evidently had no idea of leaving. In the morning his old car was still in front of Mr. Peregrine's house.

But we had another problem. Tim didn't seem to be really sick, but he kept throwing up. Sonny said he threw up the night before, too. It might have been all that unaccustomed ice cream. I got the thermometer, and he didn't have any temperature, so I knew it wasn't serious enough to need a doctor. That's what Mama always says. But it was inconvenient, to say the least. We even had to put George in the washing machine along with Tim's sheets. It didn't hurt George —whatever happened to that rabbit had to be an improvement.

But the poor kid needed to be able to eat. We gave him lots of Cokes and orange juice, because the doctor always tells Mama to give us liquids when we're like that to keep us from getting dehydrated. Tim managed to keep those down, all right.

Bob was worried though. So I said, "Why don't we

go and ask Mrs. McHenny what to do? We can say it's Sonny who's sick to his stomach."

"Good idea, Debbi."

Sonny said in that case he was going to have all the Cokes he wanted, too.

We found Mrs. McHenny in what she called "the dumps." She wasn't whittling and she wasn't drinking beer. Maybe she really could take it or leave it alone. She was on her stoop stringing beans, but not as if she was enjoying it. She usually enjoyed whatever she was doing, so this wasn't a bit like her.

"What's the matter, Mrs. McHenny?" Bob said as we went up the steps. "You look miserable."

"Yes, ma'am," I said. "You sure do."

"Well, you might call it that," Mrs. McHenny said. "I'm evicted, that's what I am. It's enough to make a lady miserable, don't you think?"

I wasn't sure what evicted was, but it did sound awful. Bob knew though. "You mean they actually said you've got to move?" he said sympathetically. "How much time did they give you?"

"All the time in the world wouldn't do me any good. I'll never find another house I can afford, where I can plant beans and tomatoes and things to eat. The social security Mr. Mac left me won't go far enough to pay the rents they charge these days, much less leave anything for beer and skittles." That was her name for what some other folks call "vittles." Vittles are food, Bob says, but the right way to spell it is *victuals*. Funny.

"I declare, sometimes I just feel like giving up," Mrs.

McHenny went on. "Mr. Carson says he's selling all this land around here to somebody who wants to make a shopping center out of it. In this little bitty town— a shopping center?" She sighed. "Well, I reckon the Lord will provide, but He better get started at it. He's only got two weeks."

I wanted to tell her one of Aunt Cammie's pious mottoes, *God helps those who help themselves,* but I thought it would be cruel right then, so I didn't. After all, I kept hearing on TV about all the people who were out of work. It wouldn't help much to have a lady as old as Mrs. McHenny added to the ones who were looking for jobs. At least she wasn't looking. She wasn't keeping anybody else from getting a job. And she did work in her garden, raising stuff to eat.

Bob said, "Is that place where those people were living—where we went the other day—is it vacant now?" He was being careful not to let on that he knew where Clay and Adele were. "I thought it looked vacant when I went by there yesterday. Maybe you could move in there if it's not on Mr. Carson's land too."

Mrs. McHenny brightened up right away. "Bobby, you might have a great idea there. I think they've left, and I don't believe it's Mr. Carson's property. Of course, it's just a shack, but it's better than nothing. I could fix it up with Mr. Mac's things." Mr. Mac's things, as far as I'd ever seen, were the green flag with the gold harp on it that she had hanging over her fireplace and the knobby stick that she once told us was a shillelagh. I'd never heard the word before, but Bob even knew how to spell it. And, of course, the big glass mug. "I'll look into it. So I'm glad you came to see me," she said, already cheerful again. "Now I'll make us a cup of tea."

"No, ma'am, thank you," we said together. We'd had it with her tea; it was so strong it was worse tasting than medicine. "We've got to get back," Bob said. "We just came to ask you something. Some advice. We don't want to worry the aunts, and it's so hard to get through to them anyway. Mama and Dad didn't tell us what to do if Sonny got sick—"

I admired Bob's way of not actually saying it was Sonny who was sick.

"Sonny sick? Well, now, tell me about it. I'll go over and see to him—if you think your aunts wouldn't mind," Mrs. McHenny said quickly. As Mama says, she has a good heart.

"No, ma'am, thank you. He's not all that sick. He just won't stop throwing up, that's all. Can't keep anything on his stomach but Cokes. But he doesn't have any temperature. We just wanted to know how he can keep down some food." Bob almost panicked; we couldn't have her actually coming to see Sonny. But I could tell that Mrs. McHenny didn't really care about coming to our house after Dad had told her he didn't want her there any more. Mama had wanted to believe her when she said she could take it or leave it alone and she'd leave it alone when she was at our house. But Dad had said no. Mrs. McHenny didn't hold it against him; she said he just didn't understand about what beer did for her. But she had stopped coming. Since she was our friend, we had had to go to see her instead. Dad hadn't thought about telling us not to do that.

"Well, I'll give you some of my stomach medicine to give him," she offered now. "If he doesn't stop throwing up pretty soon, though, you better call the doctor. That's what your mama would do."

"What's in your stomach medicine, Mrs. Mc-Henny?" I couldn't help being suspicious. I didn't think Tim was old enough to drink beer. But she really did have some medicine in a big brown bottle. She poured some into another smaller bottle for us.

"It's a receipt Mr. Mac said his mother used in Ireland, green mint tea with powdered charcoal dissolved in it, and there's nothing better for stomach trouble, believe me. I've taken enough of it. I ought to know."

That didn't sound exactly as if the medicine had cured her stomach trouble for good, but I thought we could try it. At least it hadn't killed her, so it wouldn't be really dangerous for Tim.

"And if that don't stop him from throwing up, give him a sip of vinegar every five minutes," Mrs. Mc-Henny said. "If that still don't work, then you better call the doctor."

"I'm sure he'll be O.K.," Bob said, and I said, "Thank you, ma'am." Bob put the bottle in his pocket, and we said good-by.

Mrs. McHenny called after us, "You two be careful, and don't have anything to do with any strangers. I just heard on the radio about one of the kids from the deaf-and-dumb home being missing since late last night. Named Freddy Epps. Somebody got in and snatched him right out of the dormitory. Must have been a mental case—nobody with good sense would think he could get ransom for a dummy who was on the state. You two watch out. He might be still prowling around looking for more kids to do away with."

"Does she think whoever it was killed Freddy Epps?" I said as we walked home past the Institute for the Deaf.

"I hope not," Bob said, frowning. "I do wish Mrs. McHenny wouldn't call it the deaf-and-dumb home, and I wish she wouldn't call the kids there dummies. Probably they have as much sense as anybody. It's not their fault they have to be taught how to talk without ever hearing how words sound."

"And probably all because their mothers had German measles while they were pregnant," I said. "I'm glad I had my rubella shots so I won't ever have a deaf child."

"Did Betsy have German measles when she was little?" Bob said worriedly. "You don't suppose Mickey—?"

"Of course she did." I tried to reassure him, though I really couldn't remember. Mama had said Bob and Sonny and I had to take the shots because we'd never had German measles, but she didn't say if Betsy had. Anyhow it was too late to think about it now. I thought Bob was really reaching way out for something to worry about.

To take his mind off that, I said, "I know we're supposed to go back over there tonight and scare Clay and Adele some more, but what'll we do till dark?"

"I don't know about that ghost bit after all," Bob said. "You know we nearly got caught. I've been trying to think how we could manage to show the skull again without being seen ourselves and still escape, and I can't think of any good way to do it."

"Maybe it would happen that Adele would be looking toward the window and Mr. Peregrine and Clay facing the other way," I said, "and we could be outside and let her see it again. Maybe while they're still downstairs. That way, we've got the whole yard to get away in. We won't be hemmed in like on the balcony."

"Well, I guess we ought to try it one more time," Bob said doubtfully. "But it's lucky the windows are low. I'm not about to stand on any more rotten tubs. Or balconies either."

"That's settled, then. But what are we going to do until dark? Just watch the house?"

"Hey," Bob said, and his eyes got all shiny like they do when he thinks of a really great idea that would be dangerous if anybody else thought of it. "I don't believe old Clay saw our faces that day. How about if we all three go to see Mr. Peregrine this afternoon and take back the old book he lent you? Just as if we don't know he's got company. Then we'd know how Clay explained being there, anyhow."

I had to admit it was a pretty good idea. "But we'll have to at least glance at the book first."

"Right after lunch."

Bob got Tim to take the medicine—he tasted some

first himself and he said it wasn't so bad—and it may have been what cured Tim. Or maybe he was getting well by then anyhow. He kept his lunch down, and we all felt better because of that.

It was a good thing we did take time at last to look through the old book. Because it had one of the clues to the whole mystery in it, though we didn't know that at the time.

Bob found it. He was looking at the snake tempting Adam and Eve with the apple, only it wasn't really an apple, he read somewhere, because the climate over there isn't right for apples. He was wondering out loud how come the leaves on the trees and vines were always made to grow so as to cover up the way Adam and Eve would look naked.

"It's because people used to think it was a sin to be naked," Sonny guessed. "They don't any more."

"I reckon so." Bob turned some more pages, to where the Archangel Michael was running Adam and Eve out of the Garden with his sword on fire. "Hey, look. Here's something in this book!"

"A dried pressed rose?" I said. "That's nothing. Of course Rose pressed flowers in books. I pressed some myself once, in the big dictionary."

"Not the dried rose," Bob said. "Look at this!"

WHO WAS CRYING?

I looked, and so did Sonny. He said, "What is it?"

"But," I stammered, "he said she never got married! And it sounded like the truth, too, the way he said it."

Bob said solemnly, "Yes. But this is Rose's wedding invitation. See—" He read it aloud. " 'The Reverend Stanford T. Peregrine requests the honor of your presence at the marriage of his daughter, Rose Antoinette, to Mr. Merton Claymore at twelve noon on the eighth day of June, nineteen hundred and thirty-two, at St. Michael's Church.' Get it?" Bob asked excitedly. "She must have been stood up. Her mother was already dead, see, like we thought, and her father invited all the people, and then the bridegroom never showed. So—"

"You're just guessing," I said. "That doesn't explain why he papered over the doors to her room and built the high old wall around his yard. And the skull—"

"That name," Bob said thoughtfully. "Does it strike

you that Clay and Claymore might be the same name? Claymore shortened to Clay?"

"He's not old enough," I objected. "It's been—let's see—forty years since 1932. If she was going to get married then, the bridegroom would have had to be at least twenty. And Clay doesn't look sixty years old."

"This Merton Claymore could be his father, though," Bob pointed out. "And Clay could be blackmailing Mr. Peregrine because he found out about the awful thing, whatever it was, that made Mr. Merton Claymore not marry her and Mr. Peregrine close up her room. Blackmail would explain why Mr. Peregrine lets them get away with staying there. It might be a case of revenge for something that happened a long time ago. And Mr. Peregrine can't do a thing without everybody finding out everything dreadful about Rose."

"Sounds reasonable," I admitted. "But it still leaves a lot of mysteries not explained. And I hate to think Rose was all that bad. Somehow her room doesn't look like a bad person's room. Maybe she wasn't, really. Maybe Mr. Peregrine was mistaken about whatever he thought she did that was wrong."

"Don't forget the corpus delicti," Bob said. Then he gasped with excitement as a thought struck him. "The initials on the marker! M. C.! Maybe Rose killed Mr. Merton Claymore and buried him in the old Stanford burying ground—it was right convenient. Then he sure couldn't have married her, if he was dead. Maybe that was what her father thought she did that was wrong. That would explain why he walled himself in and felt too bad to be a minister any more or have any friends. Even if nobody knew, he could've felt awful about it because God knew—"

"I don't think it could have been like that. There must be some other explanation," I said. "If Rose did that, she had to have had a mighty good reason. Or else she and her father were both out of their minds."

Sonny looked a little bit scared. "Then maybe we shouldn't go over there and take that book back," he said.

"Of course we should," Bob said. "Mr. Peregrine's

O.K. I can tell by looking at him. He's not going to hurt us. It's that other one—Clay—who looks like the bad guy. He's the one to watch out for. But there are three of us, and I don't think he'd try to hurt us in the daytime. Especially since he doesn't know we're after him. He'd try to keep us from knowing everything wasn't all right. So let's go, while Tim's taking his nap, and see what happens."

"Leave the card in the book?" I asked.

"Why not? If Mr. Peregrine knows we saw it, maybe he'll explain."

But he didn't. He didn't even let us in. When we rang the bell he came to the door, looking a whole lot older than he had before Clay and Adele showed up. After we said who we were—he didn't seem to recognize us at first—he said thank you for bringing back the book, but he couldn't invite us in because he wasn't well. He didn't say a word about those two being there.

"Can we do anything for you, sir?" I asked him. I really felt sorry for him; he did look sick. "If it's your stomach, we have some pretty good medicine Mrs. McHenny made, and we'll be glad to go and get it. It really does work, if you have an upset stomach."

"Thank you, child," he said, "but I don't have an upset stomach. It's just— Never mind. Maybe some other day you can come and see me."

There was nothing to do but say we hoped he'd feel better soon, and leave.

Sonny thought we ought to let all the air out of Clay's tires so he couldn't get away when the police came to get him. But I didn't think so. I was hoping he *would* go away, and the sooner the better. We stood there in front of the old car and debated. Bob voted for the police catching Clay, "But not right now," he said. "I've got a few things to do first."

I thought I heard Tim crying, and we hurried home. But when we got to the playroom, Tim was O.K. He had waked up and turned the TV on by himself. "See," Bob said proudly, hugging the kid, "Tim's smart! Aren't you, Tim?" And Tim ducked his head and grinned. He had a right cute grin.

"It must have been a noise on TV we heard," I said. "Tim wasn't crying, were you, Tim? You aren't sick again?" He shook his head.

"Was it George crying, then?" Bob asked, doing the Uncle Robert bit, pretending that George was alive.

Tim said, "No, Uncle Wobert. George is O.K." He even seemed to be talking plainer, now that we had him cleaned up and fed. He'd be fine, if only we could keep him away from those no-good parents of his. I knew we had to do that, somehow, and I hoped Mama and Dad would agree when they got home. I was beginning to wish they would hurry back.

"We'd better check in with the aunts," Bob said, "before they start wondering what we're doing." We went up and talked with Aunt Emma and Aunt Cammie while they were fixing supper, managing to bother them just enough so they told us to get out of the kitchen till everything was ready. Aunt Emma was frying chicken and Aunt Cammie was making a cherry pie, and we were getting hungry. "I wonder if we can convince her that Gibson likes cherry pie?" Bob said. "Tim's got to have a piece of that."

"Aw, Bob," Sonny said, "you act like he's your kid or something!"

I told him to hush up. There's nothing wrong with being kindhearted, even if you are a boy.

When you're waiting, time just creeps by. After supper it seemed as if the aunts would never go to bed. They wanted to be nice to us, so they offered to play a game of setback. It's a card game they used to play when they were kids a million years ago. Sonny got out of it by pretending he didn't know the cards, though of course he did. He knew all those numbers before he was six. Bob and I got caught and had to play. We acted stupid, though, and let the aunts win, so the game didn't last too long.

Finally they said it was bedtime, and for a wonder they went too. Then it didn't take Bob and me long to get into our blackout clothes and cover our faces with soot again, after Sonny went below. He wanted a quarter, this time, and Bob gave him one. He felt pretty bad because Sonny was missing all the fun, but he knew somebody had to stay with Tim, and we could manage better without Sonny anyhow. It was hard enough for two of us to keep out of sight.

We went over the wall and down the broken limb again, with Bob carrying the ghost under his arm. "Wasn't it Anne Boleyn's ghost that appeared carrying her head under her arm?" he muttered. "I bet she didn't have as much trouble with it as I'm having with this thing. Maybe I don't want to be an osteologist after all. I'm getting sort of tired of bones."

I giggled, and Bob said sternly, "Shush! No noise now." We were nearly under the living-room window, where the light was, and where we guessed they were sitting. Again there was no moonlight—only a lot of thunderclouds—and I could hardly see Bob at all. But when he uncovered the glimmering Thing, I could see it, all right.

We heard a noise behind us, and I jumped about a foot. Bob hurried to cover up the skull, but it was only Sonny. With his face blacked.

"Go back!" Bob whispered fiercely. "You're staying with Tim, remember? I paid you."

"Aw, Tim's asleep," Sonny whispered back. "We could see from here if the house caught on fire. I'm tired of staying with him. I thought I'd just come and see how you ghosts are getting along. Besides, it's going to rain." As if the weather had anything to do with it. But a storm did seem to be coming up fast. Lightning flashes were close to the thunder; that made the storm seem more frightening.

"Bob, make him give the quarter back," I whispered. "You promised," I said to Sonny.

"Well, I take it back. Here's your quarter. I'm going to be a ghost too."

"Shut up!" Bob whispered. "They'll hear us." He gave up on making Sonny go back and moved closer to the window. We followed him. Bob was tall enough to see into the window, and I could see if I stood on tiptoe. Sonny couldn't see in at all. Served him right; he wasn't supposed to be there. Bob motioned to him to hide under the boxwood close to the house. He hadn't put on dark clothes, though his face didn't show much because of the soot. Sonny crouched down and kept still. I guess he was glad Bob was going to let him stay.

I peeked into the room. The light was dim, of course, but all three of them were there. Adele wasn't facing the window, though, so we'd have to wait till she moved. Clay and Mr. Peregrine were all right; they were near the other window talking to each other and not noticing this window at all. We could see them and hear them without their seeing us.

Mr. Peregrine was saying, sort of desperately, "I want you to leave at once. You said you had a very good reason to talk with me—you said it was about my—daughter—so in a weak moment I opened the door. You haven't told me what you came about yet, and you've been here snooping around since yesterday. I don't have visitors. I don't know why I should let you—"

"Because," Clay said, "you're my grandfather. I'm Rose's son."

THE EAVESDROPPERS CAUGHT

I could hear Bob catch his breath. And I was surprised too. He nudged me, and I nodded. It figured.

But Mr. Peregrine didn't seem to be glad at all to see his grandson. He didn't seem to want to be anybody's grandfather. He stood up and said, "Please go away. I don't want to see you. I never would have let you in if I had known." Most people as lonely as Mr. Peregrine would have been glad to see a long-lost grandson. But I remembered how Clay had beaten up Tim, and I thought probably Mr. Peregrine was right by instinct not to want to have anything to do with him. His genes were half somebody else's besides Rose's. Maybe Merton Claymore's.

"Won't you at least let me explain?" Clay said, and his voice sounded smooth and oily. "You must have cared about my mother, or you wouldn't have sent her money."

Mr. Peregrine said harshly, "A long time ago—after

her mother died—we were close. As close as any father and daughter could be. But she left me. I would have taken care of her. Of everything. But she went away. With him. Your father, I suppose."

"Can't you understand why?" Clay said.

"No," Mr. Peregrine said. He looked very old and feeble and sad. But not like he was giving up.

"She loved him," Clay said, and he made it sound awful pathetic.

"I loved *her*," Mr. Peregrine said, and he sounded even more pitiful. "He was a scoundrel. He let her think they were going to be married. He even let her have invitations to the wedding printed. I burned them, after—"

Bob whispered to me, "He didn't know she hid one in her book."

"He was weak, but would you rather he'd gone on and married her?" Adele said. "Would you rather he'd never told her he already had a deserted wife and no divorce?"

"At the last minute—and with a child on the way? He had no right to touch her." Mr. Peregrine sounded tormented almost out of his mind. He seemed to be crumpling up. "I would have managed somehow to take care of her. But she went away with him anyway. Even after she knew."

"Wasn't there less of a scandal that way?" Clay said. "She hoped everybody just believed she'd eloped. She cared about what people thought. She probably felt she'd be disgracing you to stay. She couldn't give him up, but she couldn't marry him. It was your **fault** she didn't. I wish she had. Pretended to, I mean. Then I could have had a father. It wouldn't have mattered to anybody else."

I almost felt a little sympathy for him. I could see maybe why he thought he ought to get some of Mr. Peregrine's money left to him in the will, even if it wasn't right the way he was trying to do it. Things were different about stuff like that, back a long time ago, when everybody had what they called morals. Well, nearly everybody. Or were ashamed if they didn't have.

"It mattered to me," Mr. Peregrine said. Even one person ought to count, in my opinion. "And you let her die and buried her and never let me know anything about it. I might have saved her. When she was sick you didn't give me a chance to help her before it was too late."

"You had a chance. You didn't answer her letters," Clay said.

"I wrote her—once."

"I didn't know that," Clay said. "But—"

"She probably didn't want you to know"—Mr. Peregrine hesitated—"what I told her."

"I guess you told her you never wanted to see her again," Clay said. "So she didn't want me to let you know when she was dying. She had too much pride. She never even told me who my father was. I had to guess she named me after him. She shortened your name to Perry, though she told me about you. I guess she couldn't bear for you to know when he'd deserted her."

"Deserted her!" Mr. Peregrine seemed more surprised than angry. "He didn't."

"Oh, she *said* he was dead," Clay said. "But when I got old enough I figured it out. She was too proud to tell even me that he left us. But pride doesn't pay a doctor. It wouldn't pay our rent and buy food and clothes either, all those years she had to work so hard. She died in the free ward at the hospital."

"I would have sent her to Johns Hopkins Hospital," Mr. Peregrine said. He put his hands over his face. "I ought to have tried again. I shouldn't have felt so—hurt. That was false pride too, I suppose. But you—after you were grown—you could have taken care of her. You could have worked. Don't you make enough money to—"

"I can't work," Clay said. "I'm on Army disability. I was wounded in Korea. I worked in construction before I went in the Army."

Adele broke in, "I think you owe Clay something, Mr. Peregrine. He didn't have the nerve to come to you before, not until I married him. She wouldn't let him come while she was alive, but now—" She was trying to sound nice, but if it fooled Mr. Peregrine, it didn't fool us. She went on, "All we want is to stay here and take care of you."

"I can take care of myself. I always have."

Adele didn't pay any attention to him. She went on, "Just to be a help to you, and then maybe you'd put Clay—your own grandson—into your will. You haven't anybody else." That was mean of her, to say that right out.

"Except little Tim," Clay said. He must have figured Mr. Peregrine wasn't softening up for them, but he might for a child. His voice still sounded oily, more oily than hers. "You have a great-grandson, you know. He's named for you." I remembered that *T* in Mr. Peregrine's name on the wedding invitation. They really were looking ahead when they named the child. "He looks just like my mother—your daughter Rose." That was really going too far.

But he was getting to the old man now. I could see Mr. Peregrine wanting to believe him. "A child—like Rose?" He mumbled something about at least none of it was the child's fault, and maybe he could leave a little something in trust for him, if they'd go away now and leave him alone.

It wasn't exactly any of our business, but I thought it would sure be better if he left his money to Tim instead of to that old Clay.

"But I knew you'd want to see Tim, Grandfather," Clay said. "If you saw him, of course you would—"

Bob clutched my arm. Had Clay found Tim? He couldn't have, unless Sonny had left Tim awake and he had got out and wandered over here, somehow managing to get over the wall. I imagined all kinds of impossible things. But there hadn't been time since we left Tim ourselves for anything like that to happen. And we'd have seen him.

"I'll go get him," Adele said.

But just then there was an enormous flash of lightning and a burst of thunder, and the rain came down in huge drops, blowing toward the house on a wild storm-wind.

Sonny glanced up from where he crouched and said, "Cool it, Lord!"

We could hear Clay from inside, "I'd better close the windows."

I almost panicked. "He'll see us, by lightning light!"

"Duck!" Bob said, and we scrambled down behind the boxwood on top of Sonny, who grumbled, but under his breath. Bob still had the skull, but it was wrapped up so it wouldn't show. "Maybe he won't look this way," he said hopefully.

We were lucky. Clay was in such a hurry to shut out the storm that he just slammed the window shut, without even glancing our way.

"Hurry!" Bob said.

"And do what?" Sonny asked. I was thinking the same thing, standing there uncertainly and getting wetter every minute.

"We can't miss what happens next! We've got to get inside there and see what else he's up to. You did leave Tim asleep, Sonny?" Bob seemed to have decided to let Sonny come along too. Actually he didn't have much choice; Sonny wouldn't go back.

"I'm positive that was Tim lying there asleep," Sonny said. "It couldn't have been anybody else. Besides, he had George."

"Then it had to be Tim," Bob muttered. "Come on, let's see if Mr. Peregrine left the back door open."

He had. We stood there in the dark hall, hardly

breathing. The noise of the storm covered the sound when Sonny shifted his feet. The door to the front room was open, and we could see a long slant of dim light. Somebody was coming down the stairs.

It was Adele, carrying somebody. She didn't even glance back toward us. As she went through the door we could just see that it was a kid. A kid about the size of Tim. But it couldn't be Tim.

Bob started creeping toward the door. She had left it wide open behind her. They weren't even suspecting anybody else was in the house. If we stood back in the dark—but as close as we could get without actually being in the shaft of light—we could see the whole corner where Mr. Peregrine was sitting. And if we didn't breathe or sneeze or anything, maybe they wouldn't notice us.

As Adele went in we couldn't see Clay, but we heard him say, "Here's Tim, Grandfather."

She put the kid down in front of Mr. Peregrine. He was about the same size, all right, but he wasn't Tim. I wondered why he didn't say so and tell his real name. He didn't say anything, just began to cry. Maybe she twisted his arm and threatened him, I thought. It would've been just like her. Probably they'd been beating him too.

"Don't cry, child," Mr. Peregrine said. He put out a hand, uncertainly, toward the kid.

"It's your great-grandfather, Tim," Adele said. "Come on, give him a kiss, can't you?" She lifted the kid into Mr. Peregrine's lap. It didn't look like much of a lap, kind of bony.

Mr. Peregrine put his arm around the kid like he didn't quite know how. The kid stopped crying and looked like he wanted to say something, only he couldn't. When he stopped crying he went on making a funny noise that wasn't saying anything.

All at once I knew who he was. Bob did too. He nodded when I pointed to my ears and my mouth. They had kidnaped that kid from the institute, that's what. Because they couldn't find the real Tim to use in their scheme to soften up Mr. Peregrine. I guess they'd have secretly dropped him back at the home after they got Mr. Peregrine to sign the will. And of course, a kid who couldn't talk was just what they needed.

Mr. Peregrine said, "Tim?" and touched the kid's face. The way his fingers moved, kind of groping around, reminded me of something. At last I realized what it was. I remembered things that should have made us guess. How he couldn't find the book when it was right in front of him that day he wanted to lend it to us. How he didn't recognize us at the door, earlier, until we spoke. Why he had such dim lights. He didn't know the difference.

I forgot to keep still. "Bob," I whispered, "he can't see! The poor old guy—he must be going blind—and he didn't want anybody to know it."

Well, that blew it.

Bob put his hand over my mouth, but it was too late.

"I heard something—" Adele said.

A chair scraped, and Clay came to the door, looking out into the hall. He couldn't help seeing us.

He swore and shouted, "Where'd you come from?

Who—?" He looked mean. He lunged into the hall and grabbed at Bob. Bob slipped past him like a snake and ran into the room where Mr. Peregrine was. Clay ran after him. I did too.

"Mr. Peregrine!" I hollered. "It's only us—Debbi and Bob and Sonny from next door. He's trying to—"

Bob dodged behind a big round table. If he could keep it between them, Clay would never be able to catch him. But Adele started after him too, around the other side.

Mr. Peregrine seemed to catch on to who we were. It didn't matter about the soot on our faces, to him. But we must have looked weird to the others.

Mr. Peregrine said, "You children—run and—get away." He couldn't even stand up, because the kid was scared and hanging onto his neck now.

Bob shouted, "Don't you believe what that man tells you, Mr. Peregrine! That kid's not Tim! He isn't your great-grandchild at all."

"He's Freddy Epps!" I screamed at Clay. "And you're going to get in trouble for kidnaping him!" I leaped on his back and nearly got him down. "And if you hurt Bob you'll get creamed when Dad gets hold of you." I was pulling his hair and kicking him and screaming. I guess I lost my cool, all right.

But Sonny didn't.

Sonny stood right there in the doorway and said in a deep voice, like somebody in a TV western, "Stop right there. Everybody. If you don't—I've got my dynamite here—and I'm going to throw it! And blow you to pieces!"

GETTING THE DROP
ON THE BAD GUYS

Everybody froze. Then Clay whirled around to see who was talking. He was cussing, I guess it was. At least we had never been called that before.

I don't remember how I got back to the door, but I was there with Sonny and Bob, who had moved back around the table, facing the rest of them.

I didn't see how that thing Sonny held could fool them; it just looked like a big brownish firecracker without any fuse. It didn't look like it could blow up anybody, which is what dynamite is supposed to do.

But Clay had turned a sort of pale green color. I could see his face change, even though the light was dim. He looked really scared. He said, "It *is*—it's dynamite. Watch it, kid! *Watch* it!" in a soft yell. That is, it would have been a yell except he seemed afraid to even speak out loud. He almost whispered, "If you jar that thing the least bit it might blow us all to—"

"I know," Sonny said sweetly. "It's rather old dynamite, and old dynamite blows up easy."

Bob hadn't believed it when Sonny had told us he found his dynamite after the men got through blasting rock for the basement of the new school. He thought Sonny was putting us on, and I did too. But now he believed it, I could tell. I remembered Clay had been a construction worker; that was how he knew the real thing. So I believed it myself. I turned pale when I thought how lucky we were that it didn't go off when the tree limb broke that night.

"Be careful, Sonny!" I said anxiously.

"I am," he said tensely. "You don't have to worry, Debbi. Bennie and I watched how they handled it while they were working on the school blasting. When you're in charge of dynamite, you don't let it go off unless you're ready to. Like I might be ready to any minute now," he added, looking threateningly toward Clay.

Bob said, "I'll take over now, Sonny. You run home and phone the police, quick. Tell them these guys are the kidnapers they're looking for. The kid has to be Freddy Epps, the one Mrs. McHenny said was kidnaped from the institute. So give me the dynamite, and I'll hold them here while you—"

"Sorry," Sonny said definitely, keeping his hold on the dynamite. "You don't know how to handle this stuff, Bob. You go phone them."

"Don't fight, kids," Clay was imploring. "I tell you, if you drop it we're all—"

Bob knew how stubborn Sonny could be. "O.K.," he said. It was no time to throw his weight around as the oldest. "I'll phone the police myself. They probably wouldn't believe you anyhow."

As we'd guessed, Mr. Peregrine didn't have a phone. Who would he ever want to call up? Bob had to go to our house, to the kitchen extension, which was farthest from the aunts, so they wouldn't hear him. It didn't take him long, and he parked the wrapped-up skull while he was at home, too. Knowing Bob, I guessed he even checked on Tim.

All that time, Sonny had held the stick of dynamite ready to throw. I was scared his arm would get tired. Clay tried to sweet-talk him, but he was afraid to grab Sonny and risk his dropping it in the scuffle.

So we all stayed right where we were until Bob got back, dripping wet from the rain. The only one who had kept talking was Mr. Peregrine, and now I knew why he was asking what was going on. He couldn't see.

"Never mind, Mr. Peregrine," I said. "Sonny has been doing field research on dynamite. He's holding these two people up with a stick of it till the police get here, but he won't throw it unless they give him some trouble. And they don't want to die."

"This child—" Mr. Peregrine said helplessly.

"They took him from the Institute for the Deaf to try to fool you into thinking he was your great-grandson. They thought it would soften you up. They want your money."

That was when Bob rushed in, saying, "The police are on the way! Good work, Sonny!"

"Good work, Bob!" Sonny said, imitating him. I

could tell Sonny wasn't going to be fit to live with after this episode.

"Good thing the aunts were asleep," Bob muttered to me. "So was he." Naturally he wouldn't mention Tim's name where Clay and Adele might hear him. "And it was time we called in the police. Since the kidnap angle developed, they probably won't investigate anything else."

A big clap of thunder shook the house right then, and lightning forked across the dark piece of sky we could see through the window. Clay turned even paler. I could see him thinking even the jarring of the thunder might set off the dynamite. And I suspected it could. I felt cold all over. But there wasn't anything else to do but let Sonny hold it as a threat.

"Why don't they hurry?" I whispered to Bob. "Did they say they would?"

"Sure they said they would."

Clay made another try. "Look," he said to Bob, "you seem like a reasonable kid. Call off your brother and let us out of this. We'll give you—"

Sonny said between his teeth to Clay, "Shut up." He hefted the stick of dynamite as if getting the feel of it to throw, like a pitcher does a baseball.

I had the strangest feeling when he said that. None of us had ever said shut up like that to a grownup. I was sort of surprised—maybe I was glad—to know you could. And get away with it. Not that we ever would—unless we had some powerful weapon like Sonny had and unless they knew they deserved what we could do with it.

Bob said, "You can't bribe me, Mr. Clay Perry. You're a kidnaper and a child-beater, and the longer they keep you in jail the better."

Adele said, before she could think not to let on, "How'd you know about— Clay, he knows about—"

Bob had let it slip. But maybe, I thought, it was too late for finding out about Tim to do them any good.

I was saying silently to myself, Come on, you cops! Come on!

But all that happened was more thunder and lightning. I couldn't help feeling sort of sorry for Clay when he snarled at Mr. Peregrine, "Man, you're some grandfather for a guy to have! Look what you got us into. All you had to say was, 'Welcome home, Grandson, I'm so glad to see Rose's son.'"

See, he'd said. He hadn't realized yet that Mr. Peregrine was nearly blind. And it might be just as well not to tell him.

"How do I know you're who you say you are?" Mr. Peregrine answered weakly. "The child turned out not to be—"

I wanted to tell him then that he really did have a great-grandchild named Tim. But of course that wouldn't do, with Clay and Adele listening. And I knew I felt sorrier for Mr. Peregrine than for Clay. After all, there was no excuse for Clay to beat Tim like that.

I heard the police siren at last—and even while I was feeling relief, I was hoping it wouldn't wake up Aunt Cammie and Aunt Emma. (It didn't. They slept through the whole exciting night. That was one advantage of their being deaf.)

Clay heard the siren too. He looked around like a frightened rat in a trap.

Adele screamed at Clay, "What do we do now?" She sounded mean. She was like saying it was all his fault that the only choice they had was to get blown up by a child with dynamite or get put in jail by the police for kidnaping.

Clay just cringed. There wasn't anything he could say. Or do.

Until just at that minute, in a big clap of thunder and a crackling explosion of white lightning, all the electricity went out and we were left in pitch-black darkness.

THE YELLOW-RABBIT
HIDING PLACE

"Oh, be careful, Sonny!" I begged.

Sonny kept his cool; he didn't drop the stick of dynamite, and the lightning didn't set it off either. (Sometimes I wonder about that dynamite. But when the police got hold of it, they treated it just as respectfully as Clay had.)

In the dark we could hear Clay and Adele scrambling. I thought they were probably both trying to get out the same window. They couldn't get out through the door without bumping into us, and they were still afraid to touch Sonny and the dynamite. But the sound of the siren made them desperate, and they instinctively seized their one chance to get away. Maybe they forgot about the high stone wall and the locked gate. Maybe, I thought, they didn't realize our fallen tree branch was like a ladder that could be used to get over the wall.

Bob rushed to the front door to alert the two policemen who were there by now. "They got out the window! They may still be in the back yard!"

"They may be in our yard, next door!" I said. "They can climb over the wall—if they find out how!"

But they weren't that smart. The policemen with their flashlights found them and brought them back into the house just as the lights went back on. The power company works fast sometimes, though once when there was an ice storm we didn't have any electricity for a whole day. Sonny gasped when he saw the pistols; it was just like on TV.

"Where's the boy they kidnaped?" one policeman said to Bob.

Bob pointed to Freddy Epps, who was still hanging onto Mr. Peregrine. I went over to them and told Mr. Peregrine, "It's the police, sir. They've got Clay and Adele for kidnaping Freddy from the Institute for the Deaf. They'll take him back now. He'll be all right. And you won't have any more trouble from those two."

"What happened to the dynamite?" Mr. Peregrine said feebly as the other policeman took Freddy from him. Freddy cried, but nobody paid any attention to that. There was too much else to do.

"Yeah," the policeman who was doing the talking said. "That the kid with the dynamite?"

Sonny gave it to him, though he did look sort of stubborn and I was afraid he wasn't going to.

"You're lucky this didn't go off, son," the policeman said seriously. "Don't you know better than to play with stuff that's this dangerous?"

"I know how to handle dynamite," Sonny said, ad-

ding "sir" when he thought about being polite and realized he was talking to a policeman. "And I wasn't playing!" he couldn't help pointing out. After all, they wouldn't have caught the kidnapers if it hadn't been for Sonny. And Bob and me, too, of course.

"That's right," the policeman said, smiling a little. "It was right cool of you to threaten them with it and hold them for us. Thanks. But I bet your dad's going to tan your hide for having that stuff! Even if it turns out to be a dud. I'll try to persuade him to go light on you, though. You ought to get some kind of credit for helping the law. Where did you find the dynamite, anyhow?"

"And what were you all doing here this time of night?" the other policeman said.

"Why, we just came over to help Mr. Peregrine," Bob said innocently. "We live next door. Those two were giving him a hard time. And when we saw the kid, we suspected it was the one who had been kidnaped."

Sonny said to Bob, "Aren't you going to tell them about the sk—?"

Bob thought fast and covered the slip, saying quickly while I gave Sonny The Look, "The school? Yes, sir, that's how he found the dynamite. When they were starting the new school building, the construction crew left it after they blasted, and Sonny picked it up. We didn't believe it was real though." Sonny shut up when he caught on that Bob wasn't ready for them to know about the skull. He wasn't going to give anything away. And when Bob didn't say anything about Tim, Sonny and I didn't either.

But as soon as the policemen left with Clay and Adele and Freddy Epps, saying they'd be back tomorrow to make out a full report on everything that had happened, I said to Bob, "What about—?"

Mr. Peregrine was looking very bewildered and very old and tired too. Bob said, "Not now." Then to Mr. Peregrine, "Why don't you get some sleep, Mr. Peregrine?"

"I suppose that would be best," Mr. Peregrine murmured. "I do feel exhausted by all this . . ." He stood up. I didn't know whether or not it would be kinder to let him know we realized he couldn't see very well. I didn't know how to say it, so I didn't.

"Good night, sir," we all three said at the same time. I couldn't help adding, "We'll have a surprise for you, tomorrow morning early!" I just knew he'd be glad about Tim, his real great-grandson.

Mr. Peregrine smiled faintly. "It's been a long time since anybody said that to me. You're good children. Thank you for—for coming over to help me."

But it wasn't very early the next morning that we could take Tim over to see him. Aunt Emma took it into her head that it was time to clean up Sonny's room, because Mama and Dad were to be home the next day, and she told me to help him. My room looked all right, and so did Bob's, but she knew Sonny's was always like a disaster area.

"Couldn't it wait till this afternoon, Aunt Emma?" I said. "There's something else I've got to do this morning."

But Aunt Emma was in one of her firm moods, and she wouldn't let us put it off.

"There were some men here a while ago who wanted to see you all before you got up," she said. "I wouldn't let them in, of course. But they might come back. You go right upstairs and get that room looking decent before you do anything else!" she ordered me and Sonny.

"See you in about four weeks," I told Bob, groaning. "Come on, Sonny. This is all your fault for leaving your stuff thrown around like that." I knew the men must be from the police, or else from the newspapers if Sonny was going to be a hero. But good old Aunt Emma hadn't heard a thing they'd said. She'd got rid of them, all right.

"I'll be getting Tim ready," Bob said, low so the aunts wouldn't hear. "He needs a bath anyhow."

"His clothes are in the dryer."

"Are you calling your brother a liar?" Aunt Cammie said, looking shocked. "Debbi, I'm ashamed of you, using such language."

"I didn't, Aunt Cammie. We aren't even allowed to call each other stupid. I said he should put his clothes in the dryer!"

"She said let's have a fryer for lunch, sister," Aunt Emma said. "I declare, these children never seem to get enough fried chicken!"

"That's right, Aunt Emma," Bob shouted. "Let's

have a fryer! You do cook the best fried chicken!"

We got away, leaving them happily planning to cook us plenty of fried chicken before they had to go back home and leave us to Mama and Dad.

"Bob," I said, before Sonny and I went upstairs, "something's still bothering me. What are we going to do about the skull?"

"I don't know," he said. "That's why I didn't want Sonny to let on to that policeman. It might get Mr. Peregrine in trouble. I've been thinking, if he can't see, why was Mr. Peregrine poking around in the graveyard as if he was looking for it?"

"Well, he can see a little bit," I said.

"I bet he was just trying to be sure it was still covered up," Sonny said, "so nobody'd ever find it. Only it wasn't, because Gibson and the rain—"

"Well, we're on his side. And if he doesn't want anybody to know, he must have a good reason. Even if it's just that the scandal might get out about Rose. It couldn't do anybody any good to know after all this time."

"I don't understand about Rose," Sonny said. "I couldn't hear it all very well, under that window. This guy Clay said she was his mother, right? But he said she wouldn't tell him about his father. And Mr. Peregrine said she never did get married. So . . ."

I tried to explain it to him. "In the old days, everybody thought it was scandalous if a man and a woman lived together without being married. Now only some people still think it's a sin."

"Do we?" Sonny asked.

"I guess so. At least, I would if it were Betsy and Joe. Wouldn't you?"

"I don't know." I could see Sonny trying to imagine how it would be if Betsy and Joe hadn't got married. No wedding or anything. And still—Mickey. It's something to think about.

Bob said, "At least we know now that crying we heard was Freddy, not Tim."

I got back to the skull. "It might be against the law not to tell them about the skull," I said.

"I'm going to wait till Dad gets back to decide."

"I don't think you'd better tell Dad," Sonny said. "He's going to be plenty mad about the dynamite as it is."

"I guess I'll have to decide by myself then," Bob said. "I'm thinking about it practically all the time."

"I wish we knew for sure if it's Merton Claymore's," I said, "and what happened to him. That might make it easier for you to decide."

Well, we found out all about it. But not till later.

As soon as Sonny and I could get his room in shape, we hurried down to the playroom. Bob had Tim all slicked up, dressed in his own clothes again because Sonny's old ones were much too big. But at least his clothes were clean now. And Mr. Peregrine couldn't see well enough to notice what he had on. George had got dirty again since we washed him, but of course Tim had to take his old rabbit along anyhow.

"The aunts are still in the kitchen," I told Bob. "So we can sneak Tim out and go to Mr. Peregrine's front door."

"Right."

Mr. Peregrine invited us in and didn't even notice Tim at first. As soon as we all went into his living room he told us, "The policemen have been here this morning, children. Reporters were with them. They wanted to talk to you. I'm afraid they'll be at your house, too. I believe you told me your parents aren't home yet?"

"No, sir—coming tomorrow. Unless what they read in the papers makes them come sooner. But won't the cops have a time making the aunts understand!" Bob laughed out loud. "I think the reporters must have come early this morning. Aunt Emma got rid of them."

"Aunt Cammie and Aunt Emma are deaf," I explained to Mr. Peregrine. "They'll misunderstand if the policemen try to ask them anything. They think we were in bed all night. They'll tell the reporters we didn't have a thing to do with it."

"I told them almost everything," Mr. Peregrine said unhappily. "I told them the man said he was my grandson, a relative I didn't know I had. And that they said the child was theirs. But I let the police think they were lying about—about his being my grandson, and just trying to get money from me. It's easier if they think that. After all, the crime they're arrested for is kidnaping; I didn't prefer charges against them for anything they tried on me."

"Maybe they won't bother you any more," I said. He seemed so upset I wanted to make him feel better. "Here's the surprise we had for you, Mr. Peregrine!" I moved Tim close to him, lifted his thin bony old hand, and put it on Tim's head. "Here's your real great-grandson! And his name is Tim. That much was true."

"What do you mean? How could you—? How could he—?" Mr. Peregrine wasn't as happy as I thought he'd be. "How do you know he's my great-grandson?" he wanted to know. His hand moved over the child's head, his fingers took a wisp of Tim's reddish hair between them. Maybe it felt the way Rose's used to feel.

Of course, we didn't actually know. All we could do was guess. "Well," Bob said, "he's their real kid, anyhow—the one they had before they did the kidnaping. I was snooping the other day near the shack they were living in and saw them beating him. When they went away and left him tied up like a dog or something, I untied him. And he wanted to come with me, so I took him home. We've been taking care of him in our basement playroom, and his cuts and bruises are almost well. The aunts never caught on; they don't know a thing about him."

"Cuts? Bruises? They were hurting the child?" Mr. Peregrine looked properly horrified.

"He says his name is Tim," I said again. "Maybe Rose made them name him for you."

"More likely Clay and Adele thought about Mr. Peregrine's money, even then," Bob said, "and named him that to get next to Mr. Peregrine sometime, even if Rose wouldn't let them right then."

Mr. Peregrine was touching Tim's face with his hand now, and for a wonder Tim was letting him. "I wish I could see," he murmured. "Children, my eyesight has been getting worse for a long time. I've tried not to give in to it. I've tried not to let anyone know. I can get along all right here where I know where everything is. But I might as well admit now that I'm nearly blind. Tell me what this child looks like. What color are his eyes?"

"He has blue eyes," I said eagerly. "And reddish hair and fair skin and a few freckles."

Mr. Peregrine nodded. "Rose had a few freckles, right across her nose."

"That's where Tim's are!"

"There are laws against child abuse," Mr. Peregrine said as he stroked Tim's hair. "I've heard of such people, though it's hard to believe. The authorities wouldn't let those two keep him, of course. But—I—don't know. How can I ever be sure—?"

"Only if you feel it in your heart," I said anxiously. "Don't you?"

He still looked uncertain, longing to believe but not quite able to. It must have been very hard for him, all that happening at once. I said to Tim, "Go on, Tim, hug your grandpa! He's nice—love him! Put George down and hug him hard—"

"George?" Mr. Peregrine looked startled. Old people, I've heard, remember very clearly things that happened a long time before. "George? It can't be," he said almost fearfully, as if he hardly dared find out. "Is George—a yellow rabbit?"

Tim didn't know what to do. Mr. Peregrine didn't look much like he wanted to be hugged right then. He looked excited, squirming his hands together nervously, and at the same time he looked like he might start crying, the poor old man.

"Yes!" I said, just as excited as he was. "At least he used to be yellow, before we put him into the washer." I took George from Tim and thrust him into Mr. Peregrine's unsteady hands. Tim started crying then, but Bob put his arms around him and shushed him. Everybody was very still. Sonny even stopped chomping on his bubble gum.

"I gave Rose a yellow rabbit when she was three years old," Mr. Peregrine said in a faraway voice. "She named him George, and she loved him more than any toy she ever had. All her childhood. He was like a person to her. I never noticed if she—took George with her when she—went away."

"Tim," Bob said, "where did you get George? Tell Uncle Robert where you got him?"

"G'amma," Tim said. Grandma. Of course. Rose had kept her precious toy—I was glad she hadn't let old Clay have him when he was a kid—and had given him to her grandchild. They had Tim before Rose died. And she must have loved Tim. I bet they didn't beat him when she was around.

Mr. Peregrine's two trembling hands were feeling the dirty little stuffed rabbit all over, as if he were trying to recognize something special about him. His watery blue eyes were looking somewhere else, somewhere far off.

Then while we watched—and even Tim was quiet, his eyes big with wonder about everything that was happening—Mr. Peregrine found a place on George's stomach that had been sewed up. He put a finger into it and felt around. "If only it's here—" he muttered.

And sure as if I'd had ESP, I knew he was going to find it inside George, whatever it was.

THE MYSTERY
OF MERTON CLAYMORE

It was there, all right, deep in the stuffing. Mr. Peregrine fished around until he found what he was looking for, and we held our breath while he pulled it out from George's insides.

It was an ivory rose.

The trembling old fingers held it so tenderly I wanted to cry. He felt with his fingertips how it was carved. It looked just like a real rose, a pale yellow one. "Oh, it's so beautiful!" I said.

"I gave it to my Rose for her birthday—when she was six," Mr. Peregrine said. "She showed me once where she kept it hidden when she wasn't wearing it. Yes, this is her George, all right. And this is the right Tim—"

Mr. Peregrine was sort of crying, but he smiled too. When he held out his arms, Tim suddenly left Uncle Robert and went to him, grabbing him around the knees until Mr. Peregrine lifted him onto his lap. He gave George back to Tim, and then held him tight.

They sat there hugging each other and not saying anything. We just watched them and smiled.

After a while Mr. Peregrine said, sort of fiercely, "They hurt him. They can't have him back. I want him—but—"

I knew what he was thinking. He could manage by himself all right while the world was going black to his eyes, because he knew where everything was. But how could he take care of a kid?

Then I remembered Mrs. McHenny, and I knew it was fate that had evicted her from her house, not Mr. Carson at all. And the Lord was going to provide!

I said, stammering in my rush to assure Mr. Peregrine that everything was going to come out all right, "You can get Mrs. McHenny to come and keep house for you and look after Tim! She needs a place to stay —she's being evicted—so it'll work out perfectly. Tim will love Mrs. McHenny. We all do."

Bob and Sonny both started telling about her, too, all of us talking together. We told him everything about her except the beer. But we were sure she was telling the truth when she said she could take it or leave it alone. And we were positive she'd take good care of Tim and Mr. Peregrine. And Tim could still see Uncle Robert every day.

"Sonny will stay with you and Tim while we go and get her, won't you, Sonny?" Bob said.

"O.K.," Sonny said.

"I'll stay. You two go," I offered, because I really wanted to. I was so glad for Mr. Peregrine.

"I wonder if the court would make me his guardian,"

Mr. Peregrine said. "If his father and mother are indicted for kidnaping—well, I'm surely his next of kin. I'll get a lawyer. It doesn't really matter if people know I have a no-good grandson. This is more important. But maybe it can be private after all."

"My best friend Stephen Lee's father is a lawyer," Bob said. "They're probably home from Florida by now. My dad will be home tomorrow, too, and we'll get Mr. Lee to come and see you about it. He'll do it any way you want, and he won't tell anybody but the judge, I'll bet."

"See, everything's working out just fine," I told Mr. Peregrine.

Bob said, "We'll get Mrs. McHenny," and he and Sonny took off.

Mr. Peregrine leaned back in his old dusty velvet chair, still holding Tim tight, as if somebody might try to take Tim away from him. Tim didn't seem to mind.

"It was all my fault," he murmured. "It doesn't matter what people think. If I hadn't been so stiff-necked she might not have—"

"You couldn't help feeling hurt," I said. "We heard what they said; we were outside the window before the rain started. We know about it. But it was all just a—a misunderstanding." He didn't get mad because we had eavesdropped. He knew I was trying to make him feel better. He still looked sad and troubled, even though he was glad to have Tim. He sighed, and sat there for a while, not talking, just cuddling Tim, which was comforting for both of them, I could tell.

"Debbi, child," he said then, "will you do something for me?"

"Of course, Mr. Peregrine. I will if I can."

"I—I was so unforgiving. I wouldn't answer her letters. She wrote me a good many times. I—I wish I had answered. Oh, I kept on sending her money from time to time, after I found out where she was, until the post office began years ago to send the envelopes back with 'addressee unknown.' But I only wrote her once—to tell her something very important. She answered that letter, and kept on writing for a while. She always thanked me for the money. But I was so hurt that she had left me like that, I told her in the one letter I wrote that she was no daughter of mine any more, and that I never wanted to hear from her again. After a while she believed me. It wasn't true—God knows I did want to hear from her. I was such a fool. But she was foolish too. I know now it doesn't matter about other people. But she thought it did. We could both have lived here, behind this high wall, and the rest of the world wouldn't have mattered. Maybe her son would have turned out better— Things might have been different—"

He was wandering away from what he had been going to ask me. "What did you want me to do for you, Mr. Peregrine?" I asked, gently, when he stopped blaming himself for a minute.

"I—I kept all of Rose's letters. I couldn't bear to throw them away. Oh, I read them. I couldn't send them back unopened, though I thought about it. But I had to read them. I had to keep them. Now it's too late for me to read them over again. But I'd like— I wish I could. To see again what she said. She always ended them with 'I love you.' So, Debbi, would you read her letters aloud to me?"

I swallowed hard. I was about to cry. "Of course I will, sir," I said. "But maybe it would be better to come back this afternoon and do it? It's nearly lunchtime and the aunts will be looking for us. And here are Bob and Sonny and Mrs. McHenny. So I'll come this afternoon, O.K.?"

"Yes," he said. "Come this afternoon. Please."

It didn't take Mrs. McHenny long to move in. Her government check had just come, she said, so she could hire a man to bring her stuff and Mr. Mac's things. Mr. Peregrine wanted to pay for it, though. She and Mr. Peregrine seemed to get along fine, and Tim liked her right away, after Uncle Robert told him she was O.K. and she shook hands with George and promised to sew up his stomach.

She was already cleaning up the kitchen when I went back that afternoon. Bob and Sonny came with me and asked if Tim could come over and watch TV, and of course he could.

So there were Mr. Peregrine and I, sitting in the dusty velvet chairs in the living room. I felt sort of strange, as if I were a visitor and ought to be wearing a dress instead of my regular shorts and shirt.

He was holding a leather-covered box on his knee.

"Here are her letters," he said. "All I have left of Rose. Debbi, I'll be obliged if you'll read them to me."

"You have Tim," I reminded him. "They aren't all—"

"That's right. It's good to have Tim." He handed me the box. "I'll never feel right about Rose, though. But I'll do the best I can to make it up to Tim. I wish I could make it up to Rose."

"It wasn't your fault, sir," I said again. "Quit blaming yourself. She was the one who chose to do what she did." Whatever it was. I couldn't help wondering about the skull.

"Well, let me hear her letters, please, Debbi."

I arranged them by the dates of the postmarks. They were sent from Atlanta, with no return address. I opened the first one, feeling as if I were doing something I shouldn't be doing, seeing that yellowed paper and the slanting faded writing of a girl who had lived here in this house, slept in that rose-papered room upstairs such a long time ago, and then had gone away from it and had written back to her father:

> Dear Papa,
> I am sorry to go this way. But I have to. It would disgrace you if I stayed. I love you.
> Rose

"Mr. Peregrine," I said, "are you sure you want me to see what she said? It seems to be—sort of private."

"You won't tell any gossiping busybodies."

"No, sir, I won't." It was like taking a vow of poverty or chastity or whatever those old vows were of. As solemn as that.

Most of the letters just said she was well and hoped he was. None of them told him where she was. They all ended just like he said, with "I love you." She really did love her father. I didn't see how she could have gone off with that Merton Claymore, not if he was anything like his son. But then, I've never been in love. I guess it must make a difference.

Then there was a longer letter, dated several months after the first. I guessed—after I started reading it— that it was the answer to the one he wrote her that he said was so important. I read:

> Dear Papa,
> I'm glad you found the address in his wallet and wrote me what happened. I knew he had a heart condition, and his dying wasn't your fault. He had no business going to bother you about money, and arguing with you and getting so mad the way he always did. He knew he ought to keep quiet. I begged him not to go. You did the best thing, after it happened.
>
> I feel better, of course, because you did read the service for the dead over him when you buried him in the graveyard, and I'm sorry you had so much trouble about a marker, going so far away to get one made so that nobody would know about it. He could have done without a marker. You needn't have bothered at all, and you were good to do it.
>
> If nobody knows about it now, please don't ever let anybody know. He was an orphan and there's

*nobody to wonder what became of him. He didn't
even know where his wife is.*

*I never would have asked you for anything. You
shouldn't have sent me this money now. I'll work
and pay it back when I can. I guess I'll have to use
it, because it's nearly time for the baby and I need
it so much. Thank you for sending it. I wish you
wouldn't say you never want to see me or hear from
me again. I wish I could start over and not cause
you so much trouble and disgrace. I love you.*

Rose

I felt so sorry for her—and for him. But I felt excited too. I would never let Mr. Peregrine know I
understood what she meant, of course. But it gave us
the clue we wanted. I put two and two together and
now I knew.

I didn't say anything about what she had written, but
just kept on reading the letters, and he didn't explain.
The rest of them only thanked him for the money and
hoped he was well, except the one that told him the
baby was a boy. Then she stopped writing. There were
thin envelopes addressed to "Mrs. Rose Perry" and
stamped "Return to Sender. Addressee Unknown." I
knew each must have a check in it, written so long
ago. Had he worried about her when he lost touch with
her? Though he had told her he never wanted to see
her again? I wondered if he had told her he boarded
up her room and papered over the door when he wrote
to tell her what he had done with Mr. Merton Claymore.

But I was sorrier for Mr. Peregrine than for Rose.

He still had to live with what had happened, **and she** was out of it. He had been miserable about Rose ever since, and troubled about M.C.—he had kept on going back time after time to be sure the grave hadn't been disturbed.

"That's all the letters, sir," I said softly. I went and put my hand over his; it was the only way I could sympathize. "Do you want me to bring Tim back now?"

He sighed. "Thank you, child. Yes, I'd like to have Tim. When the cartoons are over."

I left him with the open box of letters, his hands turning over the different envelopes that all had love in them.

When I got home our house was full of reporters and photographers. They wanted a picture of Sonny with the dynamite, but the police had taken it away. So one of them made up something for him to hold that looked like a stick of dynamite. And they didn't even guess a thing about Tim! Bob had been very clever to leave him in the playroom watching TV. The aunts didn't know why they were taking Sonny's picture until they read in the paper that he had helped capture the kidnapers. They still didn't understand how he had happened to be over there next door as well as asleep in his room, and I don't guess they ever will.

After we got rid of the reporters and talked to Mama and Dad on the phone (they had just heard about it on the radio and called), I took Tim back to Mr. Peregrine and Mrs. McHenny and went home to eat supper. I was trying to decide whether I could tell Bob and Sonny what I had found out from the letters. Bob was dying to know, but after all, I had promised not to tell. Well, what Mr. Peregrine actually had said was, "You won't tell those gossiping busybodies." That surely wasn't Bob and Sonny. They'd never tell anybody.

We let the aunts know we were going to play in the yard until dark. Out under the oak tree, Bob said, "Come on. What did she say in the letters?"

"Well," I said, "I won't tell you what Rose said, because I promised Mr. Peregrine not to. But I'll tell you what I figured out happened. I know for sure whose skull it is."

"Whose?" Sonny said.

"You won't tell? Either of you? Ever? Not to anybody?"

" 'Course not."

"Me neither."

"Was it M.C.'s?" Sonny asked.

"Yes! When Rose was about to have the baby, Merton Claymore came here—it must have been late at night when nobody could see him—and got in to see Mr. Peregrine. Rose didn't want him to come, but he thought because of the baby he could get money out of Mr. Peregrine to help her."

"Just like Old Clay," Bob said. "Funny to think he was ever a baby."

"Did Mr. Peregrine kill him?" Sonny said. "He had a pretty good reason there—"

Bob looked worried. He didn't want to go to the

police about the skull. "If it was murder . . . " he said slowly.

"No, it wasn't," I told him. "Mr. Peregrine didn't kill him. They had a sort of fight, and Merton Claymore had a heart attack and died. He already had a heart condition. Rose knew about it. So guess who buried him secretly in the old family graveyard and read a service over him and didn't tell anybody because he didn't want to have to explain what Merton was doing there?"

"I was afraid it was him," Bob said unhappily. "But being a preacher at the time—and burying him in a real graveyard and reading a funeral service over him and putting a marker—maybe that made it O.K."

"Nobody knew Merton had come except Rose, and nobody missed him because he was an orphan and had no relatives and his wife was already out of touch," I went on. "When Clay said his father had deserted them, he figured wrong. Though Merton probably would have. Rose just never told anybody, not even Clay when he wondered. But she knew what had happened and she didn't blame her father a bit for concealing it. She knew he would have suffered if people had said things about her. So Mr. Peregrine just built a wall around his place and stopped having any friends so nobody would ever be in his yard looking around. He gave up being a preacher because he felt too awful about it all and probably thought God didn't approve of what he'd done. That night we saw him he was just trying—blind as he was getting—to be sure the skeleton was still hidden underground. All those years he must have kept on going out there and looking, over and over, wondering if it would show up sometime."

"And then Gibson dug it up!" Sonny said.

"The rains had already washed most of the dirt away," I reminded him.

Bob said, "Well, Dad always said we have to decide for ourselves if anything is wrong or not. And he said how to tell is to ask ourselves, Will it hurt anybody else? I think it would hurt Mr. Peregrine something awful if anybody found out about Merton Claymore now. And it might hurt Tim, too, later on. I don't think it would hurt anybody at all if nobody found out after all this time. If we three swear never to tell, nobody will ever find out."

"I'll promise," I said quickly.

"Me too," Sonny said. I was proud of him. He wouldn't tease Bob when Bob was so worried about what to do.

"As soon as it's dark," Bob said, "I'll sneak over there and bury the skull again where it was. Deep, so Gibson can't ever dig it up."

The tree limb's been moved from the wall now, and we go through the front door when we go to Mr. Peregrine's to see Tim or to bring him over here with us. Mama and Dad thought it was great how we helped capture the kidnapers, and they didn't fuss at Sonny much about the dynamite, but I don't think they quite realized what it was all about, even though

we did have to confess about keeping Tim. They didn't blame us for that. Stephen Lee's father had Clay and Adele sentenced for child abuse as well as kidnaping, and he got Mr. Peregrine appointed Tim's guardian. Mrs. McHenny takes good care of the two of them, even though she does have a beer out of the glass mug now and then.

And Betsy and Joe came and brought Mickey to see us as soon as they could, so Uncle Robert was happy about that.

But sometimes I see Bob standing by himself at night at the window, looking over toward Mr. Peregrine's field where the graveyard is, and I know he's not thinking about Tim or Mickey or about being called Uncle Robert.

My brother Bob still has a secret.

So do Sonny and I.

OTHER CAMELOT BOOKS TO ENJOY

THE VELVETEEN RABBIT by Margery Williams
THE SUMMER OF THE SWANS by Betsy Byars
AFTER THE GOAT MAN by Betsy Byars
THE HUNDRED AND ONE DALMATIONS by Dodie Smith
FINN FAMILY MOOMINTROLL
and the entire Moomin series by Tove Jansson
MATTHEW LOONEY AND THE SPACE PIRATES
by Jerome Beatty
HANG TOUGH, PAUL MATHER
and other baseball titles by Alfred Slote
RIFF, REMEMBER by Lynn Hall
THE MOUSE AND HIS CHILD by Russell Hoban
SWEETWATER by Laurence Yep
TUCKER'S COUNTRYSIDE by George Seldon
DORP DEAD by Julia Cunningham
MY DAD LIVES IN A DOWNTOWN HOTEL by Peggy Mann
THE REAL ME by Betty Miles
THE SECRETS OF HIDDEN CREEK
and other mystery titles by Wylly Folk St. John

For a complete Camelot Books catalog, please write to the Education Department, Avon Books, 959 Eighth Avenue, New York, New York 10019.